Jean Middlemas

Baiting the Trap

Vol. I

Jean Middlemas

Baiting the Trap
Vol. I

ISBN/EAN: 9783337049683

Printed in Europe, USA, Canada, Australia, Japan

Cover: Foto ©Andreas Hilbeck / pixelio.de

More available books at **www.hansebooks.com**

BAITING THE TRAP.

BAITING THE TRAP

A Novel

BY

JEAN MIDDLEMAS

AUTHOR OF "LIL" AND "WILD GEORGIE"

IN THREE VOLUMES
VOL. I.

LONDON
CHAPMAN AND HALL, 193, PICCADILLY
1875

CONTENTS.

BAITING THE TRAP.

CHAPTER I.

HAZE IN THE HORIZON.

"'A GREAT city is that which has the greatest man or woman.

"'If it be but a few ragged huts, it is still the greatest city in the world.'

"I wonder if it would be so very difficult to be great! What do you think, Margaret?" and a young girl who had been crouching for some time past, reading attentively in the window-seat, threw down her book, as the gathering shadows of evening rendered it impossible to see any longer, and walked up to the fireplace where her elder sister was sitting knitting, or rather, thinking, for frequently the click of the needles stopped, and her work fell in her lap. She started as though returning from some far-off dream, as these words fell on her ear, and evidently desirous of chasing away all sadness from her face and voice, answered cheerily, smiling the while,

"To be great one must strive continually to be good, my darling."

"You are wrong," replied the young one musingly. "Good people are often very insignificant, while wicked people are very great."

The elder sister sighed softly.

"And which are the happier, Pettita?"

"Happiness! Oh! she is a very fickle lady who only allows herself to be caught occasionally; besides, what is one person's happiness is another's misery. You and I, Madge, though we are sisters, should never seek it at the same source."

"No, child, perhaps not; yet God knows, my happiness is entirely merged in yours."

"You are a dear, good old sister, my beautiful Madge, but I wish you were not quite so fond of me. It is very nice to be coaxed and loved and petted, called baby names and all that, but it holds me back, Margaret, that you must allow; and now that I am quite eighteen, and no longer in swaddling clothes, I confess I should enjoy a little more liberty."

"The child does not know what she would have," murmured the other softly; "liberty for a woman is the road to ruin."

"Dear me, Margaret, these are really old-fashioned notions. Who would ever imagine that you were only five years my senior; to hear you talk one would think you had been a contemporary of your own grandmother? I cannot think what has made you so prematurely old."

The other did not answer at once, but rose from her seat, and walking to the window, looked out at the dreary winter landscape which was gradually fading away in the darkness.

Care had made Margaret St. Orme what her younger sister called "prematurely old." She was of a somewhat thoughtful temperament, and though her nature was placid and unexcitable, yet the troubles and worries of life did not pass lightly over her; they seemed to sink deeply into her mind, to be brooded over in solitude and dwelt on till the worst was made of every little annoyance. And she had already had her share of this world's trials, nor, she feared, was her burden in the future likely to become a lighter one. She was the sole friend, adviser, and guardian of the young, impetuous, wayward sister, who, she foresaw, would never view life from her quiet aspect. Pettita would forget the unpaid washing-bill which haunted Margaret's sleepless pillow, while she kicked rebelliously against the bounds of her little country home, and longed to see what the great world was made of. Their mother had died when Pettita was a baby, but she had never missed a mother's care, for the elder and more thoughtful sister had always been there to watch over her with the tenderest devotion. Their father, too, who had only been dead about six months, had always made an idol of Pettita—she was so like her mother, who, with her wild fitfulness, her grace, and her bright sallies had charmed him in the days of his youth; so he made a companion of his elder daughter, whose character was of his own type, and between them they spoiled Pettita, and strove to shelter her from every side-wind which could even momentarily chill the sunshine of her young life. But she was too impetuous, too instinct with strong feeling, to bask contentedly in perpetual brightness;— to some natures storm-clouds are a necessity.

Lavater has truly said, "He can bear his griefs in silence who can moderate his joys," but to Pettita both were impossible. She must indulge to the fullest in the extremes of grief and joy, and the placid monotony of Woodlands, as the tiny cottage was called where the sisters still dwelt on

after their father's death, was little in
accordance with Pettita's developing cravings
to know more of life.

"Have I vexed you, Madge?" she cried,
when the silence had lasted some minutes,
"or have you some new trouble that you
are afraid to tell me? Those dreadful bills,
haven't you paid them all yet?"

"Never mind the bills, my pet; leave
me to arrange them. Come upstairs and
look at your dress; let us see if we cannot
make even a black dress pretty, for I think
you may go to the New Year's party at the
Squire's. It is so kind of Mrs. Leigh to
offer to take charge of you."

A bright colour mantled Pettita's cheek,
while her large brown eyes flashed, and
there were angry tones in her answer,

"No, I cannot go to that party. Why
should I? If it is not decorous that you
should go out in mourning, neither will I.
Because I am a baby, I suppose you will
answer. That is just what I complain of.
I hate to be petted and fooled, Madge,

and I wish with all my heart it was stopped."

" My dear child, I thought you wished to go, and you always profess to like Mrs. Leigh."

" Mrs. Leigh ! Oh, yes ! she is charming, she is kind and pleasant and full of fun, and moreover she is quite ready to concede to me the right of having a will and a way of my own, which is more than most people do."

" A will and a way of your own, Pettita ? Why, I don't think you are ever thwarted. It seems to me that you do too much as you like, my poor child."

" Oh ! I pick what flowers I choose, have what playthings I prefer, ride the donkey about the lanes for any given number of hours that please me ; tease you, you good-tempered old saint, whenever I feel vicious ; in fact, the more I behave like a spoiled child, the better I believe you are pleased. But if I live to be as old as Methusaleh I don't think you would ever give me credit for being otherwise than a baby, or being capable of caring for anything but the most puerile of amusements."

Margaret looked fairly bewildered as she asked,

"And this tirade is all called forth by—"

"Knowing you are fidgeting over the butcher's bill," cried Pettita, laughing.

With a sudden change of humour which was one of her peculiarities, she had seen the comic side of their squabble, and accepted it at once. But the elder sister, though better read, was far denser in many ways; a rapid conclusion was the last thing she ever arrived at.

"Butchers' bills—Mrs. Leigh—a baby—and being very great! my dear Pettita, it is such a complicated puzzle, that I cannot put the pieces together."

"Well, dear, then come and sit cosily down by the fire and I will explain it. First of all, I have greater faith in myself than you have in me; next, though I cannot worry over horrid figures and un-receipted bills as you do, I should like to help to find the money to pay them. Then Mrs. Leigh put it into my head that if we went to live in London, an opportunity might offer of doing something. I over-heard her saying the other day that it was a pity a girl with my capabilities was condemned to spend her life among country bumpkins; so you see, though I am only a baby in your eyes, other people speak of me as a girl with capabilities."

"Pettita, child, you take my breath away. What does all this mean? You—my little sister—why what could you do?"

"Yes, your baby, Madge dear, would like to do something. She cannot bear to see you wearing your heart out over farthings any longer. It is such small work, Madge, this grizzling and scraping and managing; it would be so much greater to strike out a line of one's own, and thus satisfy the hunger of both mind and body at one and the same time."

Margaret sat down and looked, but did
not attempt to speak, and as the fire
flickered up and cast a gleam of light on
her face, its expression of sorrowful surprise
filled in the words her tongue refused to
utter.   Hers was a beautiful face.   She had
exquisitely chiselled features, soft, sweet,
and Madonna-like, with sad grey eyes which
told their own tale of patience and lasting
endurance, but she wholly lacked the
passion which was continually bursting
forth in Pettita, nor could she comprehend
its surgings, or follow its sudden storms
and vagaries.

She had, however, grown somewhat accustomed to outbreaks which she was wont to
consider as the mere youthful effervescence
of a spoiled child, and which she strove to
calm in her gentle loving way, but this
sudden determination, as she deemed it, to
do something for herself, fairly took her
aback ; and though she scarcely realised it in
its entirety, yet a cold sensation circling
about her heart seemed to sicken her,

as she cast the foreshadow of trouble in the future.

In a moment Pettita was on her knees, resting her arms in her sister's lap, and looking up, her bright face all aglow with enthusiasm, into the sorrowful eyes which were regarding her so lovingly.

"Yes, it is true, Madge, quite true; I have been thinking about it for a long time. I must do something. I cannot bear this dronish life any longer; patching and mending and contriving may form your sum total of existence, but it does not suit me. Let us give up this cottage and go away."

"And should you have no regret about leaving a home where you have lived so long, and where we received our dear father's last sigh?"

"Oh! please don't ask me to think about that; it only makes me feel wretched. We cannot be always 'harking back,' you know, we must go on."

"And I might then have saved myself much sorrow and pain. I dreaded to tell

you, Pettita, what I have known for some
weeks past, — that we *must* leave the
cottage."

"Hurrah!" cried Pettita, "when, and I
suppose I ought to ask, why?"

"Because we have not money enough to
stay here. It was a struggle when papa
was alive, to help us, but since his pay has
stopped it is impossible."

"Well, unless one has a large fortune, it
is better to have no money at all. Making
money must be more amusing than pinching
and saving."

"Pettita, my darling, you don't know
what you are talking about."

"Yes I do. At all events, let us try.
We cannot be worse off than we are now,
and we may improve our condition."

"And how do you intend to carry out
this money-making scheme of yours? May
I not be allowed to help?" and Margaret
smiled as she smoothed the girl's hair back
off her brow.

"Always incredulous, Madge. Well, I

hope you will live to have more faith," said Pettita, jumping up. "If you wish to know my intentions, I mean to go on the stage."

Margaret gave a faint low cry, and caught hold of the arm of her chair, as though in sudden pain.

"Never!" she exclaimed. "My father's daughter—his youngest—his pet—to walk a common stage! No, child, it is impossible. I will never sanction it. Why, he would come back from his grave to ask me if this were the way I fulfilled my trust, when in his dying hours he committed you to my care."

Pettita began to laugh hysterically. She was considerably touched by her sister's emotion, though she did not care to show it.

"Bravo, Madge!" she cried; "I am delighted to think one can excite heroics in your usually unimpressionable nature, but I hope you will calm down again and leave that field to me."

"You are very foolish and naughty," answered the other, striving to overcome her momentary excitement with an effort. "I ought to have known you were only trying to frighten me, for, after all, you don't know how to act."

"Don't I? 'Some are born great, some achieve greatness, some have greatness thrust upon them;' now I feel that I was born great," and she began to strut about the room in a mock tragic manner, which would have been very amusing to any one but Margaret. "It is no use to combat Fate," she went on; "the old hag is stronger than we are. Now, tell me, when do we leave the cottage?"

"On the 25th March."

"Another three months,—what a bore! and then we shall go to London, shall we not, Madge?"

"I don't know. I had thought of taking lodgings in the county town."

"In the county town? Oh, no!" she pleaded. "I cannot go there. There is a certain amount of freedom here, but among the gossiping nonentities we should find there, one would be driven mad. No, let us go to London."

"I doubt if we can afford it. We shall have to live in such a very poor way."

"Oh! we'll do something; take in plain needlework or washing. Better that than the stage, eh, Madge?"

"Foolish Pettita! But why should we go to London? we know no one there."

"So much the better; there will be charm in the novelty of having new acquaintances. There is Mr. Griesnach, that friend of papa's whom we have never seen; he will introduce us."

"Life is rose-coloured at eighteen," quoth Margaret soberly.

"And dun-coloured at three-and-twenty, you dear old croak. Now I am going upstairs to burnish that fusty black dress, for as we are really going away, perhaps it would be as well to show one's self at the Squire's party."

And the elder sister was left alone, for she seemed too much absorbed by her thoughts to follow Pettita forthwith. She feared, she scarcely knew what; that Pettita would really go on the stage she scarcely for a moment deemed likely, but that she would do many rash and foolish things she felt very sure. It required a great deal of consideration before she decided on taking this impetuous girl to London. Yet the very Mr. Griesnach of whom Pettita had spoken was the man to whom her father had bade her address herself in any difficulty, and perhaps, who knows, he might prove a very efficient help in directing a young untutored character.

Captain St. Orme, the father of these two girls, was a naval officer who had married a beautiful but penniless foreigner with whom he had become infatuated during a sojourn at Lima, and from that hour his life had been uphill. At her death, when Pettita was yet a baby, he settled down on his half-pay in a country cottage with his

two little girls. Though Margaret was
still very young, she was thoughtful and
somewhat precocious for her years, fond of
her father till it became almost a worship.
Thus she soon learnt to help in the house
and to initiate herself in all the minutiæ
of their straitened circumstances; and
as soon as she was old enough took so
thoroughly upon herself the smoothing
and the hiding of money difficulties from
the two beings to whom she devoted her
life, that they were neither of them fully
aware how hard was her task, or with what
patient heroism she fought bravely on.
Captain St. Orme had insured his life to
provide a miserable pittance for his children,
but it was so small that poor Margaret
was almost hopeless now, and felt the
loneliness and responsibility of her position
the more, because she was resolved, if possible, to spare Pettita. She judged the
young sister from her own standard, and
forgot to take into consideration that she
would never brood over troubles or torture

herself with misgivings as she did. While
Margaret would have found happiness and
content in a quiet unruffled life, Pettita
delighted in turmoil, excitement, and variety.
Money, of course, she wanted; money she
must have, but she probably would not be
so scrupulous as Margaret was as to the
source from whence it came. More brilliant
and attractive than her elder sister, she yet
lacked the delicacy and purity which per-
vaded all her actions; and though by the
many Margaret would perhaps be scarcely
as much appreciated as Pettita, yet "Il
semble qu'estimer quelqu'un c'est l'égaler à
soi," says La Bruyère, and those who, like
herself, loved refinement and the pale steady
light of virtue, felt that there were few
women in whom it shone so unflickeringly
as in Margaret St. Orme.

CHAPTER II.

THE CLOUDS LIFT.

AND so Pettita went to the party at the Squire's, which, after all they said, was only to be a gathering of very young people round a magnificent Christmas-tree, whereon the good-natured Squire had promised to hang many and beautiful presents, " therefore it was nonsense to be so scrupulous about the mourning; it was not often she got a chance of amusing herself." The Squire was a bachelor in declining years, but he loved to see merry joyous faces round him, and was very good and liberal with his gold; he had, however, only a life-interest in the property, and could will nothing.

c 2

away, or doubtless Margaret St. Orme would not have been forgotten, for, as he often said in his blunt way, " she was a young woman for whom he had a great respect." Had he known half the secret troubles her pride bade her conceal, probably many a bitter moment would have been spared her. Pettita he treated as every one else did, as a baby and a pet, brought her lovely boxes of bonbons whenever he went to Paris, and made pretty speeches to her when he met her in the lanes, so she stigmatised the Squire in her own mind as an ' old driveller,' and troubled herself very little about him. Lately, however, he had had a niece staying at ' The House,' as his abode was called by the country people, and she had proved rather an attractive ally of Pettita's. She was the widow of a Colonel Leigh, who had died in India two years previously; and though she was about eight-or-nine-and-twenty, she was so much younger in her ideas and habits than any one Pettita was accustomed to associate with, that for the time she was very much taken up by this new friendship, being as it was too the first reaction after the wild grief into which her father's death had plunged her. Mrs. Leigh was just the sort of person a young untutored girl would go mad about, for she possessed a certain charm which fascinated every one more or less. She was not exactly pretty, but she was graceful, well-made, and a perfect woman of the world; she had evidently studied the art of pleasing, for she always managed to say just the right thing, and had never been known to utter a discourteous or disagreeable remark to any one, though as to the innuendos she made about her friends when they were not present we will not now inquire. Truly, however, Bertha Leigh was a woman of wonderful talents, who might have been a second Chevalier d'Eon had the diplomatic requirements of the day offered a field for her services. She could not help it, poor thing! it was her misfortune and not her fault

that she had been born with the bump of
intrigue so fully developed, and that struggle
against the feeling as strongly as she would,
it yet was utterly impossible for her to do
a straightforward action or to speak the
plain unvarnished truth. Why she had
come down to visit her uncle in his country
quarters, no one quite knew, for Mrs. Leigh,
though not rich, had a snug little house in
London, with her brougham and other comfortable addenda. She had too her court
of admirers, out of which the gossips of
society had not yet been able to select the
favoured one; the truth being that she
feared to lose the mass by seeming to prefer any single individual; and Bertha
Leigh could not bear it to be said that
there was any man of her acquaintance, at
all known or sought after in London circles,
who was not more or less her slave. It
was an uncertain homage this which she
prided herself on commanding, and must
have cost her as many hours of annoyance
as of pleasure; but woe to the luckless

man who failed in his allegiance, and ten-
fold woe to the woman for whose sake he
was faithless to this self-constituted queen
of fashion. Bland words and sweet smiles
would doubtless mask her intentions; but
Mrs. Leigh would ere long find some under-
hand way of wreaking her small vengeance
on one or both. A few strong-minded individuals had marked her as dangerous, and
sought to keep themselves or their belong-
ings out of her power ; but ' public
opinion ' was with her, she was *the* most
charming woman of her set, so the one
voice was silenced by the many, and
Bertha Leigh still smiled, showed her white
teeth, made new proselytes of both sexes,
and prospered. She had taken to Pettita
St. Orme the first moment she saw her ; she
was young, impressionable, and there was
something in her ; besides, every flower
that blooms in a wilderness is a rose, and
Mrs. Leigh was sadly in want of congenial
society during her country visit. She began, therefore, to practise her little arts on

Pettita, dazzled the girl by her conversation, won her by her kind sweet manner, and filled her head with thoughts about the future, as she talked to her of London and its pleasures. She must have had misgivings though, sometimes, if she ever thought of moulding Pettita entirely to her will; there was a flash in those young eyes which, to one knowing character as Mrs. Leigh did, must have forbade her to think of coupling bondage with Pettita's name —she might be dazzled for a while, but free will must conquer at last. Strange that Bertha Leigh studiously avoided Margaret, —she would come to the cottage door and call Pettita out to walk with her, but she would rarely if ever risk an interview with the elder sister; there was evidently something in Margaret's upright straightforward character which was thoroughly antagonistic to her,—a look in her clear true eyes which Mrs. Leigh did not care to face oftener than the exigencies of society absolutely required. Thus it happened that Margaret knew comparatively little of Mrs. Leigh, and, therefore, was incompetent to form an opinion as to the advantage to be derived from the warm friendship thus suddenly sprung up. From a worldly point of view it was very desirable, she supposed; but Margaret was too unworldly herself to make much point of the matter either way, and the good old Squire's niece she accepted on his account as more than a fitting companion for Pettita. The outbreak about London and going on the stage had somewhat alarmed her, but no more had been said about the matter, and she had well-nigh forgotten it. Was Pettita beginning to be infected by some of Bertha's manœuvring ways, that she had been so reticent to her sister, fearing that by drawing the cord too tightly it might snap? When Margaret watched her depart for the Squire's party, a week had nearly intervened since their conversation, and yet it had never been alluded to again; and Pettita was a little chatterbox, and not wont to keep her ideas and feelings to herself; true, she had Bertha Leigh to open her heart to, and she was probably a more sympathetic listener than the staid, sober Margaret.

Arrived at the Squire's in the little brougham which he had sent to fetch her, Pettita at once went up to Mrs. Leigh's room. There she found her surrounded by tulle and laces, satins and velvets, powders and puffs of every description.

"Why, Mrs. Leigh, what a toilette you are making. I thought this was to be only a children's party, and you are dressed as though you were going to a court ball."

"Children grow, my dear Pettita. The people who are coming to-night have all been children once."

"Is it then a regular ball?" cried the girl aghast, as she looked at her black dress, and thought of Margaret sitting at home alone,—and she was only half delighted at having a peep into gay life.

"A little dance, my love. Three generations are to flourish under the Squire's mistletoe to-night—past, present, and to come. So the good Margaret has done the best she could for you, according to her lights, which are subdued. Bring me that box and let me see if we cannot touch up the picture, which of itself is a pretty one. One thing you do understand, child, and that is how to arrange your hair; but I strongly suspect it is its own natural luxuriance that makes it tumble about so gracefully. There, that bit of crimson and gold brightens you up wonderfully. Where has Adèle gone, I wonder? Get her to loop up your dress with the rest of those crimson flowers; then take off those horrid black ornaments, and clasp my gold ones on your arms and neck."

"Oh! Mrs. Leigh, I dare not appear dressed like this; remember I am in mourning."

"And is not black and red mourning, you profound little ignoramus?"

"What would Margaret say if she saw me?"

" Why, that she had never known before that you could look so handsome."

With flushed cheek and flattered vanity Pettita completed the transformation without expostulating farther, and then she stood looking at herself in the glass. Mrs. Leigh laughed her little soft musical laugh, and kissed the girl affectionately.

" Pleased with yourself, eh, little one? That is the first step towards conquest. Self-approval in a woman is a powerful weapon, it overturns so many barriers, and prevents one from knowing when one has failed."

" Do you possess it ? "

" No, I wish I did. I frequently doubt my power, and dread, I know not what, from others. You have not learnt yet, Pettita, what a hell of misery jealousy can evoke."

Pettita looked up in astonishment at words so unlike Bertha Leigh's usually placid sweetness. " I hope you will never be jealous of me," she said simply, while she gave the rose in her hair a twist into a more coquettish position.

A slight shiver passed over Mrs. Leigh, and dropping the hand-glass with which she was surveying her chignon, it cracked across the middle.

"Oh, I am so sorry," cried Pettita, "for it is so unlucky to break a looking-glass."

"I have broken many in my day, yet they were always evil omens," answered the other musingly; then she looked up at Pettita as though for the first time she had seen that one day the struggle between them might be a fierce one.

Tears were gathering in the girl's eyes.

"Oh! Mrs. Leigh, this has made me quite unhappy. I wish I had stayed with Margaret. I am sure some dreadful thing will happen."

"Pettita St. Orme is only a baby after all," said her friend, as though pursuing aloud the train of her thoughts, but the words at once roused the girl's indignation, and she disclaimed the appellation with warmth.

"Well, never mind, we won't think of disagreeable things any more, but go down-stairs and make ourselves as pleasant as circumstances will permit. Remember, I am your chaperone to-night, and you are not to dance with any one without my leave."

"I dare say no one will ask me!" answered Pettita, while the other smiled.

At the door of the drawing-room they met the Squire.

"What, our little wood-anemone turned into a brilliant exotic! This is your doing, Bertha, but I doubt if Margaret would thank you for it," he called out when he saw Pettita; "children should not be brought forward too soon."

To rush upstairs and divest herself of her borrowed plumes was Pettita's first impulse, but the Squire's last words checked it; she must teach these people to remember that she was no longer a child, she thought, so

she swept past the good Squire with a toss
of her head and a flash in her dark eye, and
followed Mrs. Leigh into the room. The
county families from the neighbourhood
soon began to arrive ; and as Mrs. Leigh had
predicted, it was a mixed gathering, varying
in age from the grey-haired old paterfamilias
to the fifteen-year-old fledgling, who is only
allowed to go to one or two dances at Christ-
mas time, while the governess, poor thing,
has her short infrequent holiday. The girl
looks very missish and shy in her high white
frock, and probably derives the greatest pleasure from her ball in anticipating it before,
and talking it over afterwards with her
female friends. Pettita, however, though
she had never previously been at anything
so festive, had no such misgivings—graceful
dancing and easy manners came to her as it
were intuitively, a heritage probably from
her foreign mother ; and those who had
never seen Mrs. St. Orme wondered how it
was that the girl who had spent all her life
in that poor cottage should have come out

all at once such a superb dashing young
beauty. The Squire shook his head, and
muttered Margaret's name to himself more
than once, as he watched the course of events
that night.

" She will have trouble with the child ;
would that I could help her to forego it,"
was the kindly thought, as for the first time
he became aware of the fact that Pettita was
fast unfolding into womanhood, and not likely
long to content herself with the quiet limited
sphere of Woodlands Cottage, for he did not
yet know that even that tiny home was soon
to be given up, and that a real earnest
struggle with life must ere long begin for
both of them. By the one to be borne un-
murmuringly, fought out bravely, and sancti-
fied by secret prayer ; by the other to be
combated no less determinedly, but with
bitter inward strife, and those fierce alterna-
tions of joy and grief which pertain entirely
to zealous, impetuous natures.

Pettita had quite forgotten Margaret, her
poverty, and her mourning habiliments, for

the nonce ; she was enjoying to the fullest the amusement of the hour, with that keen sense of present pleasure which so few people possess. With appreciation she was " tasting " the ruby wine, of which she would one day drink a goblet to the dregs — but not yet. Those born in affluence wander at their ease by flowing rivulets and in prolific gardens, but the poor must struggle up-hill in the heat of the noon-day sun before they reach the pleasant vineyards or can refresh themselves with the luscious tempting fruit.

> " And onward, onward, onward, seems,
>   Like precipices in our dreams,
>   To stretch beyond our sight ; "

ay, if we looked on and saw the crags from whence we might slip—the avalanches which seem ready to crush us with their weight—then would progression be indeed impossible. Pettita, however, was not likely to think of dangers or difficulties, to be either warned or frightened. She would clamour loudly over a disappointment, but gather herself speedily together for a fresh venture, while Margaret's demonstrative but perhaps deeper feeling nature would be still monotoning its patient Jeremiad.

Mrs. Leigh's injunction that Pettita was only to· dance after permission from her had been long disregarded, and there was something much resembling a wrinkle on the alabaster brow as she witnessed the admiration her young *protégée* evoked. Perhaps Bertha Leigh regretted that she had been instrumental in bringing her there — who knows ? for she echoed the general sentiment that Pettita was very lovely and dazzling-looking, and, in her winning little way, she took to herself great κυδος for cutting away the brambles which hid this pretty flower, and giving it the chance of blooming in the bright sunshine.

"How good of Mrs. Leigh to help that St. Orme girl forward ! It is more than every pretty woman would do; but then she is so unselfish, and thoughtful for others," was the remark made more than once during the evening of the Squire's party. Thus Bertha Leigh had won some of the golden opinions which she so invariably craved, though perhaps they were scarcely the extent of the stake for which she had thrown. How uncharitable, I think I hear some one observe—but was Mrs. Leigh ever known to act without a motive ?

CHAPTER III.

MAKING AN ACQUAINTANCE.

"Do leave off those everlasting accounts for a few minutes, Margaret, and let me tell you all about last night. I have been waiting vainly for a pause in that calculation of money, but you go on as though you had not already discovered that you cannot divide nothing."

Margaret closed her account-book with a sigh. She had indeed full well learnt the truth of Pettita's words, and then she walked across the room to the little sofa on which the younger sister was lounging, for it was the day after the Squire's party, and Pettita was indulging in the *dolce far niente* which inevitably follows the excitement of a successful *début*.

" Have you got anything particular to tell me, dear ? " she asked. " You look very feverish and large-eyed, as though late hours were not good for you."

" They are meat and drink," she cried eagerly. " I was so happy last night, everybody was so polite and made me such pretty compliments; you would have been quite proud of your baby-sister had you heard them."

" I am very glad you liked it," answered the other gravely, " but you must not learn to love gaiety, little one, for remember we are too poor to mix much in society, and must be content if we can maintain ourselves like gentlewomen in a quiet way."

" Then I shall live about as long as a fish in a stagnant pool; but don't you worry yourself, Margaret, people always work out their own destinies in life, and I shall not be behind mine, which I can tell you is

not to hide my light under a bushel. I
have not formed any plans yet, but I have
no doubt they will mature themselves."

"I had hoped you had given up such
nonsense, Pettita ; this wild talk makes me
quite unhappy when I think of it."

"Then don't think of it, dearest, but
listen to what I have to say about last
night. Well, the old house looked lovely,
it was all flowers, perfumes, and candles ;
everything was arranged with exquisite
taste by Mrs. Leigh, who seems to touch
things with a fairy's wand, and they instantly become beautiful. But I dare say
you have seen bright scenes like this one
Madge ; only have patience with me. It was
my first peep into dreamland, and so, you
know, I was quite carried away, and I stood
and looked almost like one entranced ; then
suddenly I wondered where Prince Charming was, for it would not have been fairy-
land, would it, without a hero? And, lo ! as
though he had been borne there by spirits
at my will, he was standing at Mrs. Leigh's

side, twirling the prettiest little silken moustache and looking for all the world just like a woman dressed up—the handsomest, half-fledged downy hero you ever saw."

" You little fool," said Margaret, laughing as the young one prattled on, " it is well your ' half-fledged hero ' does not hear you, or the down you so eloquently describe might suddenly become bristles."

" Oh! but Prince Charming was very lovely, and I am not laughing at him at all. He asked who I was. I heard him, and then Mrs. Leigh introduced us."

" Well, and who was he ? "

" That I don't know, his name was evidently intended to remain a mystery ; for when the presentation took place I only heard my own, and neither of them would tell me afterwards — they only laughed when I inquired. He wrote Edward on my programme ; fancy, we had real pink and white programmes for dancing ; but Edward is not so pretty a name as Prince

Charming, so I called him Prince Charming all the evening."

" You called a strange gentleman Prince Charming ! my dear Pettita, you surely did not so far forget yourself ? "

" What was the harm, dear ? He was only a boy, and I could not call him Edward, you know. Well, we danced and we danced and we danced till—my poor dear Madge, I am afraid there is a hole in my shoe."

" Well, if that be the most serious damage which has arisen from all this dancing with fairy princes, we will try and remedy it," said Margaret, with a serio-comic expression on her pale face, which considerably excited Pettita's mirth as she looked up at her with beaming eyes.

" I have not fallen irretrievably in love, if that be what you mean, you practical old Mentor. I have a great deal to do before that time, still I have a notion Prince Charming and I shall not be strangers in the future. He will have some influence either for good or bad over my life."

" Pettita, I shall have seriously to lecture you if you will persist in these delusions. A woman's life, child, should be spent in the magic circle of home ; even if that home be poor, it may be happy if we will only be contented, and strive to be good.

> ' My home, my home, though thou art small,
> Thou art to me th' Escurial.' "

" Very well in theory, Madge—looks well on paper and all that, but in practice I should prefer the real Escurial. I wonder whether Prince Charming lives in a palace or a cabin ? "

" Very strange of Mrs. Leigh to introduce you to a gentleman without telling you who he is. I shall ask her."

" Please don't. A strong wind will blow away my air-castles quite soon enough. I would rather not know more than my fancy suggests, for the present at all events.

To find that he were Brown, Jones, or Robinson, were a blow from which I should take months to recover myself. Call me a baby in this matter if you will, Margaret, it is only in youth that we can indulge in dreams. When I go into the world, I wonder if I shall grow staid and practical like you? You'll stick by me and take care of me if I don't, eh, Madge?"

" Whatever happens, Pettita, you know I will never desert you."

" All right, but don't let us get sentimental, it unhinges one. Who is that coming in at the gate?—a visitor I declare. I hope our only Abigail has got a clean apron, though it does not much matter, for he is a seedy looking little individual—not my Prince Charming, unless a bad fairy has transformed him."

Margaret started up and clutched the back of the nearest chair—difficulties were ever present to her mind, and her first thought was that this man might probably be some dun. To save Pettita from annoy-

ance was her next, and she at once went out
into the little passage to receive the un-
welcome visitor, if possible, alone. The
moment she saw him the ice melted from
about her heart, for she knew at a glance
that she had alarmed herself unnecessarily.
He was a little man about forty, with long
lank black hair hanging untidily about, and
keen little eyes that seemed to pierce you
through ; but as he took off his hat to
Margaret, the highly-developed head and
open brow told its own tale of mental cul-
ture, just as the sad pained expression about
the mouth told of inward conflicts and
vexations of spirit ; for patiently as he
might bear his cross, yet it could not be
borne in private. He was deformed, and to
a shy, sensitive, retiring nature as his was,
it was a bitter trial this walking among his
fellows, of them but not like them, knowing
that he was pointed at and remarked on,
perhaps jeered at and held up to ridicule by
thoughtless scoffers. Margaret had never
seen him before, but she knew at once that

he was Mr. Griesnach, her father's friend—
the man to whom she had been bidden to
address herself in any case of difficulty.
She held out her hand which received a warm
shake.

"St. Orme's daughter?" he said. "I need
not ask though, you are so like him. I
should have been here before, but have been
abroad for months, and letters never follow
me. I only heard of your poor father's
death on my return home last week."

Margaret opened the door and ushered
him into the sitting-room where Pettita was
still lounging on the sofa. She jumped up
hurriedly, and with a quick bow to the
stranger, was about to leave the room. This
was probably some horrid man about business, she thought, and from the very instinct
she had that any business connected with
them could scarcely be pleasant, Pettita
invariably shrank from facing it; but her
sister stopped her gently.

"Mr. Griesnach, Pettita; will you not
stay and speak to him?"

"Of course I will," she cried, holding out both hands in her eager impetuous way. "You do not know how welcome you are. Now you will tell us all about London?   I do want to go there so much."

He smiled, a very pleasant kind smile as he for a moment or two contemplated Pettita's radiant face without speaking, and then he looked from her to her sister, as though he were comparing them.

"I am like my mother—at least so every one says—don't look at me as if I were a stranger to you."

"I never saw your mother but once, and then—yes, the features are all there, and the—

"What I wonder," murmured Pettita to herself, as she walked away half frowning over the close inspection which she scarcely appreciated.

"Forgive me, my child," he said, following her and putting out his hand, "you were both little more than babies when I saw you last, and I can scarcely realize the flight of years; but we shall be friends, shall we not?"

"I am sure I hope so," was the ready answer; "that is to say, if you are prepared to be very nice, and to further my views. I certainly want a good friend very badly."

"Young ladies' views are sometimes rather difficult to follow," he answered, "but I will do my best when I have learnt what they are."

"Oh! you will be expected to persuade Madge there that I am a woman, and not a mere automaton to be wound up for amusement, and that I am capable of doing something to better my condition in life, which, as I dare say you know, is at present that of a pauper. In fact, instead of repining over what might have been, had the gods been kinder, I should like to obtain a position and money for myself."

"Hush, Pettita, hush, Mr. Griesnach will be quite shocked; he does not know yet how we have spoiled you, and let you talk at random as you would."

"But he does know better than either of you suspect," he interrupted. "How youthful enthusiasm will rebel against narrow limits, and how the mind seems sometimes as it were pinioned and longs for work,— active, all-absorbing work. To such ardent natures idleness is a curse, want of proper employment a life-long misery."

"But this only holds good for men," suggested Margaret, "women have, or ought to have, their avocations at home."

"There are women and women, my dear Miss St. Orme. We must discuss this matter more fully when we have learnt to know and understand each other better."

"Then you will help me to do something and to get lots of money," broke in Pettita. "Ah! don't look grave, as though you thought me sordid, but I do want to save Margaret from being worried. I do want to get money to pay the bills."

"My poor children, has it indeed come to this?" he said tenderly. But the dark

flush on Margaret's proud face showed him
that she did not thank the younger sister for
these revelations.

With tact and delicacy he immediately
turned the conversation into another channel,
though perhaps a scarcely less painful one,
for he asked all particulars about his old
friend's death, and seemed hardly less
touched than his sorrowing daughters, as he
listened to the details of how he had passed
away to his rest, grieving only that he was
compelled to leave his orphan children to
buffet, as well as they could, with the difficulties of life. A deeper interest than mere
friendship, taking the word in its accepted
worldly sense, must have existed between
the two men,—a bond of some sort of which
the girls knew nothing, or he would not
have been so overcome by grief or so readily
have pledged himself to take the father or
elder brother's place. Mr. Griesnach, however, could only help them with advice and
kindly interest, for he was by no means a
rich man himself, nor would the proud Mar-

garet have accepted pecuniary assistance had it been offered.

Richard Griesnach was a worker, though owing to frequent ill-health the time he could devote to sedentary pursuits was necessarily so small that it did not tend to fill his purse rapidly ; yet he lived by his brains, which were ever acute and busy, as is not unfrequently the case when the physical powers are feeble. He had been called to the bar in years gone by, but had never practised his profession. He kept, however, his chambers in the Temple, and wrote occasional stinging and sarcastic articles in some of the leading papers, which brought grist to the mill, but which his acquaintances could scarcely believe to have emanated from the gentle softly spoken little man, who, on the rare occasions when he was prevailed on to go into society, was never known to have given utterance to a caustic remark. Only those who knew him the best would look grave, as though they were fully aware that the inner life of this man had its dark spots—that an irritability of brain existed, which could only relieve itself in pungent satire, the heart all the while being loving, tender, and true. Mr. Griesnach had no relations—an old aunt, long since dead, was said to have brought him up. But no one knew exactly whence he came or who he was, and he never vouchsafed any information on the subject. Few, perhaps, took enough interest in him to inquire, for his bodily infirmity rendered him unprepossessing looking, and his retiring habits prevented most people from finding out what a mass of knowledge, what a keen sense of observation he possessed, or how agreeable and well read a companion he could prove. To the St. Ormes he had come under very peculiar circumstances, and they speedily forgot that he was not in appearance like other men. Margaret was fascinated by and interested in him, partly perhaps for that very reason, partly from old associations, while Pettita was ready to cling to him as the rudder which was to guide her on the perilous sea of life.

"So you give up the cottage in March. Well, after all, I think the little lady here is right, and that you had better come to London. I can look after you there."

"Hurrah!" cried Pettita, dancing round the room in her delight, and seeming entirely to forget that her new friend was but the acquaintance of half an hour.

Mr. Griesnach smiled as he sat rubbing his long taper fingers,—sunbeams like Pettita did not often irradiate his firmament.

"Not so fast, Miss—. What is your name?"

"Isabelle Mary," she answered promptly, "but every one calls me Pettita, because I am small and a pet."

"Called after your mother," he said gravely, "of whom you are the living image."

"If you only saw my mamma once, how is it that you remember her so well?"

E 2

"There are some faces, child, which leave an impression time cannot efface."

Pettita looked at him as though the matter were beyond her comprehension, and then, to Margaret's great relief, she sat down at the farther end of the room and took a book. Reading was Pettita's unfailing resource whenever she was puzzled or provoked ; she seemed to think no one would dare to interfere with her if she were shielded by literature.

"You do not share in your sister's enthusiastic desire to go to London ?" resumed Mr. Griesnach, turning to the elder girl.

"I hardly know what is for the best. I sometimes think we shall be better there, and then again I fear," and she cast a furtive glance across the room at Pettita absorbed in her book.

"Let the child make her mark if she can ; never try to hold her back," he said softly. "Guidance is one thing, coercion is another. We must hold a little committee of ways and means though, but I dare say they will not be difficult to arrange. I am afraid you will think me a horrid Cockney, my dear young lady, but in my opinion there is no place in England like London. Living in poverty in the country, or in a country town, is a sorry life, even for a woman," and he smiled as though he had already discovered how Margaret thought that a woman's lot on earth was to endure in patient privacy, and never to put herself forward to eclipse others or to assert her independence.

"I should be happier so," she answered, "but if Pettita thinks otherwise and you advise it, I will be overruled, though not convinced. I cannot but dread a life in London, yet I will never leave Pettita while she wants my protection and care."

"Then, it is decided that we go," cried Pettita, throwing down her book and jumping up. "You will never convince Margaret, Mr. Griesnach; if she says she will go without being convinced, that is quite as much as you can expect."

"I am afraid my wish to have you in

town, my dear children, is a terribly selfish
one, for though I think I can do more for
you there than here, yet the country is so
antipathetic to my own habits that I never
visit it unless compelled to do so, and never,
as you know, saw your poor father excepting
when at rare intervals he came up to town."

"How good of you then to make such a
sacrifice for us now !" said Margaret. "I
should indeed be ungrateful if I were longer
to hesitate about making our future home in
London, when so kind a friend as yourself
will be near to advise and direct us."

Thus, against Margaret's better judgment,
it was decided that they should go to London,
for, as Pettita had truly said, she seldom
changed her opinion, though she occasionally
waived it to please other people.

CHAPTER IV.

PRINCE CHARMING.

SOME men are happiest when not in the society of their own sex. Mr. Griesnach was one of these. He felt soothed by the companionship of women, he believed fully in the real or assumed interest they took in him, and imagined that they could understand him better than his sterner and more logical brethren. Perhaps there was something just a trifle womanish in the compound of talent, irritability, and kindheartedness which were his leading chaacteristics. Woman in the more intimate and sociable relations of life was what Mr. Griesnach liked. He preferred a home where

he could pop in when he felt cross-grained
and out of temper with himself and the
world generally, and where he felt sure of a
cordial reception, a gentle voice, and a patient
listener, while he dilated on his latest quirks
and fancies or, on more trying occasions,
burst out in invectives on the hard usage
bestowed on him by fate. The St. Ormes'
cottage was just the dovecot where he was
likely to nestle down and find a few peaceful
hours ; and when he had been two or three
days at Woodlands he anathematized himself that he had allowed his prejudice against
country life to stand so long in the way of
making this agreeable acquaintance. The
links, too, in the chain of pleasant associations had been considerably strengthened by
frequent meetings with Mrs. Leigh, who
had smiled her sweetest smiles on the little
deformed man, and spoken to him in her
most dulcet strains. The one crooked in
body, the other crooked in mind, who shall
prognosticate how this strangely matched
acquaintance shall end ! For the nonce Mr.

Griesnach was thoroughly fascinated. Man of the world though he was, he accepted Bertha Leigh as she presented herself, and never sought to rend the veil which hid her truer nature. She was *au courant* with all the anecdotes of the London life to which he belonged, though he but seldom abjured the solitude of his own chambers to visit it; thus they had many topics of interest in common, and she knew so exactly how to lay her little soft palm on all his open wounds and close them by the gentle pressure, that he seemed to forget himself and his infirmities when he was in her presence; and keen as he usually was in discovering supposed slights and indignities where none existed, it never for a moment suggested itself to him that Mrs. Leigh was other than the genuine kind creature she appeared, or that it were possible she could be laughing in her sleeve over the "self-sufficiency and overweening conceit of that miserable little cripple." Mrs. Leigh was too cautious to make her real sentiments known to Pettita, who really liked Mr. Griesnach, so she was compelled at times to smother them in a way that half-stifled her. Still, notwithstanding all the soft purring and graceful gentleness of this feline woman's attractions, Mr. Griesnach's favourite was Pettita; he admired her buoyancy, her spirit, her indomitable energy of purpose, and resolved to help her to the fullest extent in his power, an office in which Mrs. Leigh most fully concurred. "Between them," she said, "it would be strange if Pettita did not do something substantial for herself." Make a rich marriage, forsooth! would have been her only alternative a few years since, but women now are learning to walk alone, and they look forward as impatiently to a self-made career as does any young B.A. just emancipated from the trammels of college life. How Pettita meant to distinguish herself none of her friends quite knew. She was not as fully qualified for asserting woman's rights in the arena of physic, science, or land, as would have been her

prosier and more retiring sister, who had
read steadily all her spare hours, while
Pettita had only sipped the sweets here and
there from the books which pleased her
fancy. With all her desire for fame, she
had never been thoroughly impressed by the
knowledge that to attain it years of hard
work and unswerving patience are necessary.

"My father's daughters must not work
for their living," was Margaret's last-century
remark whenever the subject was mooted
before her, so they were all forced to leave
it with the hope that when once she went to
live in London, and saw the rapidly developing demand for women's work, and how the
barriers which had hemmed them in were
being razed to the ground, she would then
view the matter in a different spirit, and
perhaps be herself desirous of adding by her
industry to her small store of home comforts.

And so the little party went on for some
days, Margaret in her quiet undemonstrative

way doing everything that could possibly
tend to Mr. Griesnach's comfort, while, as
not unfrequently happens to calm and retiring
people, she was often slighted and overlooked
for her more rattling and piquante sister.
And Pettita had neither seen nor heard any
more of Prince Charming, about whom,
girl-like, she was beginning to feel rather
curious, and was rendered still more so by
the mysterious silence Mrs. Leigh observed
about him. It was evident she had some
design in introducing him to Pettita, and,
with her knowledge of human nature, she
calculated on interesting her more fully in
him by enveloping the whole affair in
mystery.

Mr. Griesnach and the two ladies were
sauntering through the Squire's grounds
one afternoon, Margaret, as usual, having
stayed at home to look after some household
affair, when who should be seen approaching
them but the very Prince Charming himself.
The ladies were instantly all smiles when
they perceived him, but a little frown for a

moment contracted Mrs. Leigh's brow as Mr. Griesnach exclaimed,

"Why, Bazalgette, who would have dreamed of meeting you here?"

"It is yet more astonishing to see you away from your Temple haunts, Mr. Griesnach. I do occasionally condescend to hunt the fox."

The mutual recognition of the two men evidently did not please Bertha Leigh, though she would scarcely allow her annoyance to be perceived, but said glibly,

"Then it is a coterie of friends—this is indeed charming. Have you been up to 'The House,' Edward?"

"Yes; and hearing from the Squire that you and Miss St. Orme were in the grounds, I strolled forth in search of you."

Then a sort of restraint seemed to come over every one, and no one spoke for a few seconds. Prince Charming was evidently wondering what relation Mr. Griesnach bore to Pettita. Mr. Griesnach was trying to surmise what had brought him there at all,

Mrs. Leigh was engrossed by the suspicion that he probably knew more of this youth than exactly suited her projects, and Pettita was quite blindfolded, and consequently incapable of penetrating the mystery, if mystery there were. Each, for some unknown reason, seemed to feel that the *rencontre* was an inconvenient one. Mrs. Leigh, though probably the most annoyed, was nevertheless the first to recover her self-possession.

"It is getting very cold," she observed, "January days in the country are certainly not lively, suppose we all adjourn to my little sitting-room at 'The House,' and have tea?"

"It will be too late I am afraid for Pettita to walk home," suggested Mr. Griesnach.

"Nonsense," cried Pettita, "it is not five minutes' walk from 'The House' to the cottage, and I traverse that short distance at all hours, don't I Mrs. Leigh?"

So it was agreed, and to 'The House' they went; no one thought of Margaret and her patient homely housekeeping, but round a good fire in the cosy little room which the Squire had allotted to his niece, they all four seemed determined to make themselves thoroughly comfortable, and to forget for the time, at least, whatever disagreeables might ensue. Bertha naturally devoted herself to Mr. Griesnach, and left the two very young people to resume the badinage and incipient flirtation which had begun on the night of the ball. What Mrs. Leigh's object was the sequel may perhaps show; she certainly did not make a rule of introducing her male pets to her female friends, but this was evidently an exceptional case. Sir Edward Bazalgette, or, as Pettita called him, Prince Charming was a young man of a type pretty well known about town; at Hurlingham, in the Row, he was constantly to be seen, dressed in Poole's last, glass in eye, bouquet in button-hole, lounging along as though the earth were made but for him, or driving his high-steppers in a way which showed he

was but a dandy-whip, a mere ignoramus
in the matter of horse-flesh ; but then he
was a baronet with an income, and what
matter if his mental capabilities were below
par, and his conversation never rose above
the platitudes of mere gossip ?   In the eyes
of modern society noodledom were paradise
if it were paved with gold.   Was the pro-
motion of a marriage with this youth the
substantial assistance Mrs. Leigh intended
to vouchsafe to Pettita ?   A look she occasionally bestowed on them from under her
drooping lashes, carrying on the while an
animated discussion with Mr. Griesnach,
showed that in all probability it was
not.

"Those children are really becoming too
noisy ; how fatiguing we should think it
now if we had the exuberant spirits of
nineteen !" she said at last, abruptly inter-
rupting the talk which had turned on the
Darwinian theory and was becoming too
learned for her.   Bertha never did more
than skim the surface of knowledge, nor

was she backward in announcing the fact that she had no depth of learning. Mr. Griesnach very frequently overwhelmed her.

"Yes," he said, "a few stern realities soon serve to dash the gauzy wings which would bear us into those regions of ether where we imagine the sky is always blue; but for you, my dear Mrs. Leigh, life is at its brightest. You can still laugh as merrily as those children there. Bazalgette, by the way, though still young enough, knows more of the world than many much older men."

"Then you are acquainted with his history? It is a sad one."

"I do not know to what you particularly refer. I only meant that he belongs to rather a fast set, and consequently knows more than is perhaps quite good for him."

Mrs. Leigh saw she had somewhat overshot her mark, but she instantly repaired the mistake.

"Oh! I don't know anything about him except that his mother died when he was a little boy, his father before he came of age, and it must be a sad trial to be left all alone at a very early period of existence to find out the intricacies of life for one's self. My acquaintance with Sir Edward is very slight; he seems a nice boy,—innocent I should have thought rather than fast."

Mr. Griesnach smiled. Mrs. Leigh's sense of observation was somewhat at fault, he thought to himself, but it was scarcely his province to enlighten her, so he merely asked casually what had brought the young man under discussion into that part of the country.

"He has relations living in the neighbourhood; he came partly for my uncle's little dance, and you need scarcely ask why he stays."

"Perhaps not, perhaps not. Pettita, don't you think we ought to be going home, your sister will imagine we are lost?"

In the somewhat new amusement of bandying repartee with a good-looking man Pettita had quite forgotten how late it was growing; but she jumped up at once when she heard Mr. Griesnach's words, and prepared to accompany him.

" She is pretty, isn't she? observed Mrs. Leigh as, the door having at last closed on them, she coiled herself up lazily in an arm-chair by the fire and settled herself for a *tête-à-tête* with her remaining visitor.

" Pretty! She is perfectly charming," said the other enthusiastically ; " but what has old Humpty-Dumpty got to do with her ? "

" He is the guardian appointed by the father to watch over his daughters' naughts."

" Bah! He is a horrid little brute, knows too much by half."

" That is just what he says of *you*,—yes, he is clever decidedly."

" Mere abstract cleverness. He may have as much of that as pleases him, but I

hate your shrewd people who can see
through a brick wall. So he has been passing his remarks on me, has he? *ergo*, I
suppose in future I shall be denied all speech
of the little girl."

"The pedestal on which you place yourself is not a lofty one," she answered
laughing.

"Well, you know all that hateful story?"

"Some of it — yes, but Mr. Griesnach
evidently does not, so keep your own
counsel and be brave."

"I thought Miss St. Orme was a great
friend of yours."

"So she is. Who told you she was
not?"

"Well, women are queer creatures; they
beat my comprehension altogether. Would
you like me to take a shooting-box in these
parts, Mrs. Leigh, since you seem so very
anxious that I should continue this friendship—flirtation—call it what you will?"

"No need, the St. Ormes are coming to
live in London, so you will have plenty of

opportunities of meeting at my house."
He gave a low whistle, and there was a
silence for two or three minutes.

"I think I shall go abroad," he said at
last, "England must be too hot to hold me
long. I will go wild boar hunting in
Wallachia, and send you and Miss St. Orme
the tusks to quarrel for."

"That—anything would be better than
what you are doing now; but I don't think
you will go away. You will stay on like a
moth, allured by the light of Pettita's
eyes."

"When a man tries to be moral and
respectable, society won't let him," he said
hastily. "I am not a bad-hearted fellow,
though I say it myself; and if people would
only let me alone, I should balance myself
pretty averagely, but I am always getting
pulled about first this way and then that."

"When a man has acted as you have
done, he has defied society. She must interfere; we cannot afford to let Sir Edward
Bazalgette follow the dictates of his good

heart as though he were a common tinker," answered Mrs. Leigh with more of a sneer than was usually allowed to express itself.

" Curse rank and title, why can't a fellow be allowed to do as he likes ? "

" Because so few people know what they do like, and you, my dear Sir Edward, are I suspect among the number. However, I have no wish to bias you in any way; the course in life which you choose to pursue must be a matter of indifference to me."

" Why, then, did you introduce me to that girl ? "

" Chance always plays the most conspicuous part in our lives."

" Fatalism is no doubt a comfortable doctrine if one can wholly give oneself up to it," he said moodily, half talking to himself; " for then it is not *I* but the stern arbiter of one's destiny who is to blame for what is wrong."

" You seem to be uncomfortably burdened

with a conscience this afternoon; a case of liver I am afraid, as they used to say in India."

"Pardon me," he answered, bowing gracefully. "I forgot I was talking to a lady."

She laughed joyously, not in the least offended by the rebuke.

"Do you wish to infer that women as a rule are not overburdened with conscientious scruples?"

"Some certainly are not; but may I, Mrs. Leigh, ring and order my horse? I am afraid I shall be late for dinner, which is a grievous offence with the people whose guest I am."

"We part friends, I hope. You will forgive my attack on your principles."

"Willingly, it is my fault not yours; were my principles stronger they would scarcely be so easily ridiculed."

"You are severe to-day, Ted, take care how you get into the habit of making caustic speeches; they will dash away the dew, and you will lose the boyishness which is your charm."

"Good-bye, Mrs. Leigh, a man should have something more than mere boyishness to trust to when he has reached three-and-twenty. You have taught me a lesson to-day without perhaps quite intending it, and I still think my wisest course is to go abroad."

"To pine in solitude in some wild spot over a chimera which you call principle, which a more practical person would call folly. The thing cannot be allowed, my dear boy. Dine with me this day week in Belgrave Street, when I hope you will have resumed your usual self."

Sir Edward hung his head.

"I will dine with you—yes—I do not say I shall leave so soon as that, yet I feel sure that one false step now will entail perhaps an incalculable amount of misery hereafter."

And so he left her.

"He is not such a noodle as the world

believes him to be, but he is nevertheless as weak as water," was Bertha's mental comment as she went upstairs to dress, and she smiled complacently to herself while making her toilette, in a way which showed her sharp London maid that her mistress' little plans were ripening in the sunshine of success.

No such self-complacency accompanied Sir Edward, to judge from the way he took his steed across country, back to his friend's house by the nearest route. Had he been called upon at that moment for an answer, he would have testified unhesitatingly to his hatred for Mrs. Leigh; he was never at any time one of her enthusiastic admirers, and yet she fascinated him. Weakness of purpose was Edward Bazalgette's besetting sin; he found it to his cost, and Bertha Leigh had that sort of power over him which a woman of her calibre could so easily acquire if she chose; he the while hating her more and more as he winced under her rule, though he had not the strength to free

himself from the yoke. Never before, however, had he felt so thoroughly irritated and
rebellious ; and by the time he had termi-
nated his rapid ride, he had fully resolved
to cut the Gordian knot which bound him
to troubles in England, and not to be talked
out of going abroad either by Mrs. Leigh or
any other woman.

CHAPTER V.

THE 'ARGUS.'

MR. GRIESNACH was sitting alone in his chambers, bending in somewhat moody thought over a large fire. The pained expression which at times almost passed away from his face was more strongly marked than usual, and the feverish gleam in the dark eyes plainly testified to the inward wrestle of which language scarcely avails to tell.

Though returned but a few days from Woodlands, to judge from the irritable workings of that fragile little frame, female companionship had scarcely accomplished its usual office of soothing. Alas! for him

who realises so fully how mental power
depends on physical strength, and how the
busy brain unaided by nourishment from
the body runs riot in irritability and dis-
content.

One of Richard Griesnach's dark moods
was on him now. He had fought the
demon of distrust and unbelief for hours;
he had combated despair at every issue;
large beads of perspiration standing on his
brow showed the mental torture, and he
sank back in his chair, his feeble frame
exhausted by his self-communings.

Every human being who has thought,
pulse, entity, must have a purpose for, an
object in, existence. Fame and Love are
the twin potentates who govern brain and
heart, and Mr. Griesnach would fain "fill
the empty gaps of life," but they stared
him in the face, cold, void, and cheerless.
Fame was beyond his reach; that bodily
infirmity which he ever regarded as his
curse, closed every portal to a career which,
but for this, might have been glorious and

triumphant, and he would have borne the cross patiently, ungilded though it was, had not that other gate been closed too, and he felt that with the curse of his infirmities upon him, he did not dare to ask for the love and tenderness which would have compensated for all other griefs, and, indeed have "filled the empty gaps" of that lonely troubled existence.

Have we not all gaps, some more some less, according to the amount of sensitiveness which we possess? Aye, but few, we trust, lead such an utterly cheerless, hopeless life as did Richard Griesnach, with every desire, too, to be benevolent and kindly and trustful. The self-imposed charge of the St. Ormes had, now that he had returned to the quietude of his ordinary avocations, set him off in a train of thought, and dug up old memories which, as he dwelt on them, had worked him into a state of feverish excitement. In Pettita he saw reflected all those struggling tendencies which were so strongly developed in his

own character.   There was a hungry longing
about the girl which, unsatisfied, would
starve her into an atrophy,—a restlessness
which by success alone would ever be
linked with happiness.   None of this did
the calm, thoughtful Margaret understand ;
to her Pettita's impetuous vagaries were
but the ebullitions of youth, which in a
year or two would die out, and she would
settle down soberly and discreetly as a
woman should.   But Richard Griesnach
knew better, and to assist in carving out a
happy future for Pettita was the task he had
allotted to himself, though how that end
was to be attained was the question he had
been impatiently asking himself full many a
time during the last few hours.

No practical conclusion had evidently
been arrived at,—an issue which was,
perhaps, scarcely to be expected, considering the state of fermentation into which
the good little man had worked himself.
The dark hours, however, were passing
away, and as was usually the case after one

of these exhausting trials, he was ill, feeble, and spent.

He was lying back in his arm-chair, when he was suddenly called upon to gather himself courageously together by the some-what abrupt introduction of a visitor. A fussy, pompous, good-tempered-looking man, short, and squarely built, and of a rubicund physiognomy, his hand full of papers and pamphlets tied together with ominous-looking bits of red tape, brought a chair, and seated himself at the opposite side of the fire.

"Ho, ho, Griesnach! you look ailing to-day. Afraid I have come at a bad time, but I want much to have a talk with you."

Mr. Griesnach pushed back his long hair with a weary look.

"I am not well to-day. My head is scarcely clear enough for business, I fear; but talk on, I will listen."

"Lucky dog, you! to be able to lie back in your chair and take life quietly, while your fellows are well-nigh worked to death.

Here have I been sorting papers, drawing up statistical reports, and writing letters half the night, and all the morning I have been rushing about the town like a mad bull, in search of information of all sorts, while you have been sleeping and dreaming."

"Never mind me," answered the other, wincing under the careless words; "my work and yours are of different orders."

"That is just it, my dear fellow. I cannot see why they should be though. You have brains, feeble and delicate as you look, or you could not write those stinging articles which occasionally set the people talking round every breakfast-table. Now, why should not we coalesce? I have too much work to do, you have none at all."

"Pardon me, Mr. Jenkins, but had you not better employ a machine?" suggested Mr. Griesnach, softly, though the covert sneer showed how he writhed under the coarse, unfeeling, but probably well-meant attack.

"Machine-work pays better than hand-labour in these days, my dear sir," said the man he called Jenkins, with a boisterous laugh. "Time is money, money is time, with business men; and, after all, what more do you want? We hacks don't need the tender treatment bestowed on racers, but we get our bread and cheese for all that, and many of your high-bred ones starve in the training."

"'Travaillez pour la gloire, et qu'un sordide gain
Ne soit jamais l'objet d'un illustre écrivain.'

said Mr. Griesnach, quoting Boileau quietly, but the point was too fine to penetrate Mr. Jenkins' thick hide, so he only laughed loudly and began to fuss about with his papers.

"Business, my good sir, business. I cannot afford to waste time talking nothings. Are you or are you not disposed to help me? I assure you I am overwhelmed. I am Secretary to the Committee of the Free-thought Co-operative Society, Chairman of

the Provident Association of Worn-out Literary Hacks; I have undertaken to sell
shares in the Limited Liability Knowledge-
diffusing Company; as you know, I do
articles for several weeklies and monthlies,
and it pays, my good sir, it pays. But
what is crushing me at this moment is a
letter I have received from an educational
board, offering me work of a very interesting and remunerative character. Now, the
furnace is not big enough to keep all the
irons hot, however strenuously I may use
the bellows."

"So you want me to assist in blowing?
You should have applied to some one with
more corporeal strength," said Mr. Griesnach,
half amused at this "muscular educationist,"
half annoyed by his proposition to himself.

"No, no, no; you do the sedentary part
of the work, I'll run about and bring you
information by the ton."

"And on what subject do you desire that
I should use my pen?"

"Higher education of women, my dear

sir, higher education of women," said
Jenkins, who had a trick of repeating himself; "that is the topic nowadays. Don't
agree with it in the least myself, not in the
least; but no matter, if it pays to puff it my
purpose is answered. The board wants an
organ; concentration, my dear sir, nothing
to be done without concentration; scattered
forces make no head against the common foe
ignorance. I gather them up, you manipu-
late them into a mass. Joint-stock business
—joint-stock business—I run, you write.
I have not time to write, that is the fact;
too much energy, far too much energy."

"Can I see the letter from the Board?"
asked Mr. Griesnach, to whom Jenkins'
tirade gave a very confused notion of what
was required.

"Certainly, my good sir, certainly; but as
to terms, why of course we must make our
own."

It seemed that the letter which had put
Jenkins into a greater fuss than was even
his ordinary state, was to the effect that a

pamphlet, magazine, or organ, as he called it, was required to be published monthly, which should give a statistical account of how education, that of women especially, was proceeding in the various quarters of the civilised globe; the information to be reduced to tangible shape, and offered by dint of editorial knowledge, in a readable form to the public. To collect the required information Jenkins found himself quite equal, but though he did, as he said, write articles for one or two periodicals, they were publications of a low calibre, and he did not feel that he had the head-piece necessary for carrying on and arranging this somewhat important undertaking. But he was a man of energy, who never gave up anything if he could help it. "Half a loaf is better than no bread," was the conclusion he arrived at on thinking the matter over, and if he could only form what he called a "coalition" with Mr. Griesnach, it might prove a lucky venture for them both.

Jenkins was one of the rough-and-ready

kind, who lived entirely by his wits, making the best of whatever turned up, and troubling himself very little as to ways and means. He was too go-ahead in his habits to study character, except in its merest outline, though instinct generally prevented him from being imposed upon. Delicate touches, refinement, sensitiveness, were totally lost on him; thus he was quite incapable of reading Richard Griesnach, and regarded him as a " poor devil with brains " to whom a five-pound-note was an object. Little did he anticipate then the difficulties which would be raised, before anything like a satisfactory arrangement could be arrived at. The order of things must be entirely reversed before Mr. Griesnach would listen to any proposition. Jenkins must be the machine, he himself the directing power. Intellect declined *in toto* to be subservient to mere commercial value.

"Upon my word, I never thought you would have proved such a tough customer to deal with," exclaimed Jenkins, after the

subject had been discussed for some time
very minutely, and Mr. Griesnach had
plainly given him to understand what their
relative positions must be, supposing that
he should decide to accept the editorship of
this educational organ. Interference from
his coadjutor he felt he should never be able
to brook, yet he was thoroughly aware that
Jenkins possessed the very qualities in
which he was himself the most wanting,
namely, impudence and activity, and therefore he understood that a coalition might be
effected with advantage, if he could only
succeed in keeping Jenkins in a secondary
place. Slothful by nature, and consequently
not easily roused into seizing a new idea, it
was somewhat unlike Mr. Griesnach's usual
habit thus readily to entertain the thought
of harnessing himself with an amount of
business which must be done "to time."
His writing had hitherto been of a very
desultory nature; the "genus irritabile,"
of which he was a specimen, can scarcely be
put under pressure and made to write a

certain given number of lines "to order,"
for an appointed day. But the thought had
flashed across his mind that this was an
opening which might serve the St. Orme
sisters; a magazine which was to be instrumental in raising the standard of woman's
education, could scarcely fail to produce
work for women, he fancied, and therefore
he determined to close with Jenkins' offer,
if he could arrive at an arrangement by
which that offer should be made amenable
to his wishes.

The "auri sacra fames" was not upon
him; thus he was the more likely to come
to terms with Jenkins, who worshipped
Mammon with extreme reverence. To keep
the fussy, pompous little bureaucrat from
interfering too much, and asserting his
ignorance on every possible occasion, was
the difficulty under which Mr. Griesnach
was likely to labour, especially as he would
be dependent on him for information.

It was a rash venture when we consider
that a sensitive, delicately organized, refined

man was to be brought into almost daily
working union with a coarse, rough boor,
who had, moreover, a rattling tongue and
an unfortunate habit of making blunt,
unfeeling speeches. The firm seemed ill-
assorted, taken individually, but the ingre-
dients were there which would conduce to
the public weal. None of the component
parts were wanting. Self-government in
the matter of temper was the only quality
required to balance the raft which was to
be freighted with so much nineteenth century
knowledge.

And so at last it was agreed, Jenkins
being, perhaps, the least pleased with the
bargain, that Mr. Griesnach was to edit the
'Educational Argus' in his own name, and
be answerable for what should be inserted;
he having sole power, while Jenkins, like a
faithful dog, brought the game to the bag,
and asked no questions as to its disposal.

It was a strange finale to the torturing
hours Richard Griesnach had spent; it
seemed almost as if Providence had sent

him work to make him forget himself and
his wrongs. Well would it have been had
he thus taken it, but Providence and
Richard Griesnach were too often at issue.
He had not faith enough to bear his trials
for good; like Thomas of old, he wanted
more light; what he did not see for himself
with the eyes of sense, he passed over as
superstitious folly —mere comedy to be
played out for the amusement of the weak
and the childish. " More knowledge, more
power, more love," are heart cries which
rend and lacerate, but the chilliest, the
ghastliest of all is that hopeless wail for
" more light." Here, then, was the secret
of Richard Griesnach's bitterest sufferings ;
his sole reliance was in that " ego " which
has so often sought ere now to equalise man
with God.

He sat for a long time very calmly there,
after Jenkins had fussed himself out of the
room with the promise to introduce him
forthwith to the Board, and there was a
pleased smile on his noble-looking, intelligent

face which was very different from the expression it had worn earlier in the day.

"At his age he was going to work,—to
become a drudge—for what ?   For Pettita's
sake."

The idea tickled him so much that he
actually laughed as he lay back there in his
solitude, and thought over all the different
emotions with which the morning had been
so pregnant.   That Jenkins of all men
should come to him as a Fate, an individual
for whom he had always had a feeling of pity,
commingled with contempt, as for one who,
having started in life as a barrister, had
"fallen from his high estate," and lost caste
when he took to doing hack work, and
turned bureau hanger-on for money; and
now he himself was going to join in one of
his specious undertakings.   The idea was
almost too preposterous to be true.   To
what an ebb will not circumstances bring a
man; aye, and an upright, chivalrous one
too.   There is an old saying that "you
cannot touch pitch without dirtying your

fingers," but it was very evident that Mr. Griesnach meant to prove, if possible, that he was an exception to the rule.

At length he got up, and having made a hasty toilet, and partaken of a slight repast, he prepared to start West. He had suddenly bethought himself of the existence of Mrs. Leigh, who, by this time had returned to town, but on whom he had not yet called. He would relate to her his day's experiences, and find, he in nowise doubted, a ready listener and a sympathetic adviser.

CHAPTER VI.

SHAKING THE SIEVE.

MRS. LEIGH is 'at home,' in society's acceptation of the term. It is Thursday afternoon, and after an idea borrowed from our French neighbours, she receives all those of her acquaintance who may feel disposed to wile away a leisure hour by participating in a little lively gossip. Bertha had adopted the plan soon after she took up her residence in London, because she found it was the fashion in the set into which she was herself launched, but she was beginning to find it rather irksome. Her acquaintances did not always quite amalgamate, neither did it altogether suit a woman of Bertha Leigh's

intriguing proclivities to let every one see
her hand, which was a misfortune very
likely to befall when the great mass of her
associates was brought together every Thursday afternoon; in fact, she regarded the
whole thing as a terrible *géne*, and meant to
take an early opportunity of stopping it.
Her receptions, however, were always so
crowded and brilliant that vanity had
hitherto held her back, and this, her first
reunion since her absence from town, was
likely to prove no exception to the rule.
Mrs. Leigh was fond of patronising
talent; she was fully aware that to be the
' fashion' there must be something to attract,
so she collected clever people of all sorts at
her house, both from the artistic and literary
worlds, and if she had left them to amuse
themselves and others according to their
lights, the system would have worked to
perfection; but she was always exercising
her own talents in the way of amalgamations,
rousing petty jealousies by her innuendos;
setting people who might otherwise have

been firm friends for life irrecoverably by
the ears. "Disunion is strength" was
the motto on which she ever acted ; and
though like most manœuvring people, she
occasionally pulled the cord too tightly, and
had some little difficulty in getting her head
out of a noose, yet on the whole she was
very well satisfied with her success; only
these dreadful Thursday afternoons kept her
in a state of dread lest something should
come out, some word be dropped which
should prove a key to some of her mysterious entanglements.   For Bertha Leigh, be
it known, was a shocking coward, and she
shrank instinctively from the bright sunshine; the twilight cast a much more
becoming light over her little schemes.   If
any of them had been or was likely to be
brought into day, she would shut herself in
her room and weep floods of bitter tears.
Mr. Griesnach knew nothing of Mrs. Leigh's
receptions, or he would scarcely have chosen
this particular day to pay a visit from which
he hoped for solace and sympathy; and great

was his consternation on being shown into
the drawing-room to find a small mob of
well-dressed people, talking and laughing
as if amusement were the only occupation
in life. Nor was his entrance a source of
gratification to Mrs. Leigh; she did not care
to face the remarks about 'the maimed and
the halt' with which she knew she would inevitably be assailed by various members of
that giddy throng. However, according to
her wont, she received Mr. Griesnach with
one of her brightest smiles, and whispering
softly,

"Don't mention the St. Ormes here," she
introduced him to the lady next her, and
passed on to talk to others of her guests.

Brilliant as was the assemblage, it was
evident that there were some smouldering
ashes passing about which might at any
moment burst into a conflagration, and it
required all Bertha's most winning ways
and plausible little speeches to avert the im-
pending blaze. A truculent-looking middle-
aged woman, of sufficiently offensive manners

to testify a well-established position in high society, was standing near the mantelpiece with a very ominous frown on her by no means pleasing physiognomy. She was one of those stern guardians of morality before whom frivolity quails and levity seeks to hide an abashed head. To a drawing-room like Mrs. Leigh's she was invaluable— a widow who receives, and to whom a censorious world might occasionally apply the phrase, 'Not too particular,' would make no standing-point at all if she did not cultivate a few of these unbending matrons who lead the phalanx of propriety. Her ladyship's feathers had, however, been considerably ruffled on this occasion; and though Bertha almost cringed before her, she was so obsequiously meek, yet smoothing that agitated plumage was no easy matter. At the other end of the room there was a knot of noisy talkers, towards whom the irate lady looked every now and then during her angry discussion with Mrs. Leigh. One of these was a pretty woman—a woman of whom Bertha herself might have been jealous, but against whom Lady Bluntisfield would scarcely dare to tilt, yet she evidently was the object of her indignation.

"Dear Lady Bluntisfield, indeed you are mistaken; she is my late husband's cousin. I assure you your suspicions are unfounded."

"The ebb to which modern society has fallen is a low one, I am fully aware, but I did not expect to meet people of this sort at your house, Mrs. Leigh," answered the enraged matron.

"Poor Marcia, I did not know she possessed any vice but that of being pretty," answered Bertha innocently. "Her beauty makes me wickedly envious sometimes. She is very young and unsophisticated. If you would only take her under your fostering wing, dear Lady Bluntisfield, her future would be made. This is indeed what I had hoped."

"Never, Mrs. Leigh, never. Young girls who don't know how to conduct themselves as gentlewomen, will never be patronized or

smiled on by me, and I must say it would
be your wiser course, as a young unprotected
woman yourself, to free yourself from your
acquaintance with that very objectionable
member of society."

A loud laugh from the girl called Marcia
formed a sort of echo to this speech, and
made Bertha Leigh wish that either the one
or the other of them were at the Antipodes.

"I will not encourage her to come so
often. She is somewhat noisy I am afraid,
but I thought it was rather a kindness," she
said softly.

"That young person is not only noisy,
she is imbued with an amount of vulgarity
and levity which is inadmissible in good
society. A kind heart is not always the best
monitress, my dear Mrs. Leigh."

Probably had Lady Bluntisfield been
closely examined on the subject, she might
have concurred in Fontenelle's saying that
"A good stomach and a bad heart are essential to happiness." Anyhow, she gave
Bertha Leigh credit for more self-imposed

wretchedness on behalf of other people than she at all deserved.

But honied words too often hide the void within.

A flash just for half a second broke out from under Bertha's half-closed lids; the faintest twitch played about the full lips; but she readily recovered herself, and went on with her self-imposed part.

" Ah ! well, society has its demands I suppose," she murmured softly, " and they must be paid. I know you speak because you are really interested in my welfare, dear Lady Bluntisfield, and I hope you will have no farther cause for complaint."

" But I have—I have. You are stepping far too freely on the precincts of Bohemia, —these quasi-gentry are not to be tolerated in our society. There are too many of them everywhere, but you, my dear Mrs. Leigh, should keep especially clear. Your lone position entails the greatest circumspection."

" Oh ! this is too much," thought Bertha to herself. " If life is to be all Lent and no

Carnaval, it isn't worth having," and her eye followed Lady Bluntisfield's round the room to see against whom her present wrath was directed. Her handsome tenor, the ornament of her parties and one of her especial and particular pets, was the evident victim. A woman can bear unflinchingly a merciless attack on another woman, even though she be her best and dearest friend, but to maintain a bland smile while her pet man is being censured and derided requires a consummate actress. Bertha, however, was equal to the occasion.

"Oh! he is so useful," was all she said in extenuation for noticing this *vaurien* singer; "his warbling always seems to please."

"As a paid professional he is well enough, but I am afraid he comes here on terms of equality."

"Dear Lady Bluntisfield, how you misjudge me, when you believe me capable of admitting a man like that within the pale of my acquaintance!"

"You were seen talking to him at the theatre not very long ago."

"Well, is there a crime in that?" answered Bertha, smiling sweetly, "one must be civil to the creatures who are of service to us. La Bruyère says, 'Un jardinier n'est un homme qu'aux yeux d'une réligieuse,' and professional singers have the only difference that they cultivate art instead of nature."

"Oh, if you really see it in that light, I am rejoiced, but from remarks I had heard made, I feared you looked on this man as something more than a mere voice-machine,—he is always here, you know."

"On Thursdays, yes, when he comes to amuse my friends. I hope you do not think I would admit him at other times."

"Well, don't take my friendly words amiss, dear Mrs. Leigh; I cannot, however, refrain from sounding a note of warning when I am interested in any one and see danger. Who is the little cripple who has just come in? I don't think I ever saw him before."

" A friend of my uncle's, with whom I have been staying in the country. He is a barrister, and a very clever one, too," answered Bertha promptly, giving an outlined sketch of her own about Mr. Griesnach.

"Will you present him to me?" asked Lady Bluntisfield, on whom Richard Griesnach's intelligent face had made an impression, enhanced in her mind by comparison with what she called the " puppyism of these degenerate days."

"Some other time I will with pleasure; but he is so very shy and morbid that at times I am almost afraid to speak to him myself; you must come and meet him some day when all this world is not here, then you will appreciate him fully."

Thus she artfully put off *sine die* an introduction which would in no way have suited her arrangements, and right thankful did she feel when a few moments later she

saw Lady Bluntisfield prepare to depart.
If she would only catch a cold which should
confine her in the house for months, how
grateful would Mrs. Leigh be! but no such
good luck was likely to befall, for Lady
Bluntisfield was as tough as leather, and
Bertha could not afford to offend her, so she
was compelled to parry her attacks as best
she could, and to bring all her diplomatic
art to bear in keeping matters smooth.   For
this day she trusted her work was done;
but no, just as the good lady was saying her
final *au revoirs*, the door was thrown open
and Sir Edward Bazalgette was announced.
Here was another black sheep, and, to
judge from Lady Bluntisfield's face, a very
black one, too, for she was not wont to bestow such unmistakeable marks of her dis-
approval on those individuals whom she dis-
tinguished as belonging to her own class.
She did not speak, however, only gave a
grunt and a very ugly jerk of her head,
when the young man in question bowed as
he passed her into the room.

At last she was gone, and Bertha breathed more freely; in fact, the atmosphere seemed to have become so suddenly cleared and rarified by her absence, that she became quite joyous and excited, a phase to which her usually placid temperament did not frequently rise; but she joked so familiarly with the good-looking tenor, so much pointed repartee, so many half-whispered *double-entendres* passed between them, that perhaps Lady Bluntisfield was not so far wrong in her somewhat interfering remarks. Though, after all, it was only a little way Mrs. Leigh had; she had no especial *penchant* for this particular man, but he was one of her *troupe*, and, as such she meant to retain him, and therefore employed the sort of attractions which she thought the most likely to keep him enslaved. But while this animated conversation was proceeding, Mrs. Leigh was by no means wholly absorbed by it, her eyes and thoughts were everywhere, and she saw every little combination that was being formed. If she suffered personally by these Thursday afternoons, they, at least, bore their fruit by letting her know what pairings and "coalitions," as Jenkins would have called them, were going on among her friends. Sir Edward Bazalgette and Mr. Griesnach had shuffled together she saw with an amused twinkle; that there was an ulterior motive on the part of Sir Edward she felt very sure, for his personal regard for "Humpty Dumpty" was, she knew, infinitesimally small.

"Marcia, you are not going? Do stop and dine; I shall be alone and dull," she said softly as the former passed in front of her while she was still talking to the tenor.

"Would with pleasure, dear, but I have an engagement; the governor has asked some fogies and I must preside at home."

"I am sorry. I wanted a chat; but you will come soon, love, when we can have it to ourselves. I have seen nothing of you in this crowd." And with a pressure of the hand they parted.

Which was the truth? Was Marcia Fenton

still to remain one of Mrs. Leigh's dearest
friends, or was she to be dropped to please
the great lady whom she dared not offend,
because under the patronage of her stern
respectability, Bertha was enabled to carry
on many little intrigues and practices for
which, under less powerful protection, she
would probably have been coolly treated, if
not absolutely cut, by that very fickle dame,
Society ?   To a certain extent, perhaps, Lady
Bluntisfield was right in her dislike to Miss
Fenton ; she was very noisy and off-hand,
talked slang as if it were her mother-tongue,
and was dashing and showy in her dress as
well as her manners.   She was the daughter
of a money lender, who had amassed con-
siderable wealth,—a fact which had not
reached Lady Bluntisfield, placed as she was
on that highly respectable pinnacle of hers,
but still she had not failed to discover that
the young person was very third-rate, and
did not belong to her set.   As to her being
a connection of the late Colonel Leigh, that
was a mere fabrication of Bertha's, who

never could walk otherwise than indirectly in the paths of Truth. She had only made acquaintance with Miss Fenton some months previously; and, as in many respects she suited her, they had become fast friends. Marcia had always plenty of money to command, and was ready for any amount of gadding about and amusement, only she was very irrepressible, a flagrant vice in Mrs. Leigh's eyes, and one which she vainly sought to stem, but all her little suggestions were totally disregarded. Marcia Fenton would always put herself very much *en évidence*, and be as loud and noisy both in her behaviour and attire as though gentleness and quietness were totally unfeminine virtues. She was altogether a very difficult card to play, especially when she would insist on presenting herself on Thursday afternoons, but still for all that Mrs. Leigh scarcely felt inclined to give her up. She must manage to keep on friendly terms with all these odds and ends of life, which never would fit into the same fabric. After all

how could any one imagine that they would ?
A mansion built in every style of known
architecture would be an anomaly, and
why should people of strong characteristic
types, each with a line of his own, be expected to shake down amicably together in
the same drawing-room ?   Even you, Mrs.
Leigh, with all your aptitude for *finesse* will
not manage it ; and so she thought herself
as, the crowd having departed, she stood
listening to the end of the conversation
between Sir Edward Bazalgette and Mr.
Griesnach.

CHAPTER VII.

WOMEN'S WORK.

"WERE they both going to stop?" Bertha Leigh wondered, as she coiled herself up in the corner of the sofa in a lazy sleepy fashion peculiarly her own; if so, she would have to go on acting, and the pressure had been rather high to-day, she felt somewhat weary.

"When are the St. Ormes coming to town?" she asked, putting a leading question at once.

"Not till March, I believe," answered Mr. Griesnach; "at least the term for which they have the cottage does not expire till then."

" What nonsense! you should persuade them to come at once. I hate things being put off, they lose their interest."

" Money, I am afraid, is *the* difficulty; speedy arrangements without it are not easily effected."

"I think I shall ask them to come and stay here," pursued Mrs. Leigh, looking fixedly at the two men to see if her words made any mark, " at all events I will invite Pettita. I should think she would be terribly in the way while Margaret is packing up the household gods. There are some people here to whom I want to introduce her. She must lose no time in being started. Will you back my application to have her, Mr. Griesnach ? "

" With pleasure," he answered, " if she is to come to town the sooner the better."

Poor Margaret, no one thought of her, or troubled themselves whether she came or stayed away.

" Agreed then. I will write to-morrow and you will endorse my appeal. You are going out of town, I think, are you not, Sir

Edward?" she went on, suddenly changing her tone and addressing her other visitor.

"Who? I? Ah! Yes; well I scarcely know."

"Very coherent and to the point, I must say. Like most men, I suppose, you please the fancy of the fleeting hour."

"The exception proves the rule," he answered, rising, "for I must be off. I have a long standing dinner and theatre engagement, which I had nearly forgotten in this agreeable society."

Sir Edward had had some experiences of Mrs. Leigh's banter lately, and he did not feel inclined to expose himself to more, besides he always hated to play number three. This was exactly what Bertha had wished, and she had commenced the onslaught, expecting to beat him off the field, allowing him, however, to carry the knowledge with him that Pettita might possibly come to London soon, a fact which she hoped would have the effect of keeping him on in town.

"Poor boy, he is very nice, and I am quite pleased to talk his affairs over with him sometimes, but I want so much to have a chat with you, Mr. Griesnach," she said, as the door being closed they were left alone.

"For that express purpose am I here. I suppose I could hardly have chosen a worse day."

"All's well that ends well," she answered gaily, "and now tell me all about yourself. What have you been doing since you came to town, and, above all, how are you?"

In a few terse sentences he gave a graphic account of his day's experiences.

"How clever you are!" she exclaimed when he had finished. "Ah! well, you know I am not clever in the least, and I am often thankful for it, it seems to make people suffer so much. Is not it a blessing that mediocrity has its consolations?"

"Are you not doing yourself an in-justice?" he asked. "No one surely can be kind and considerate for others as you are without at times feeling deeply."

"Oh! that is quite another thing, but if I were to put myself in the agonies of mind that you do I should not be able to console and sympathise; though I am not at all clever myself I can appreciate cleverness in others, and almost worship them for it. Acknowledge now, Mr. Griesnach, that you have antidotes to misery in those hours when we all make much of you and pet you?"

"My hours for being petted are like angels' visits," he said, smiling sadly.

"Well, come here whenever you feel dejected and unhappy, and you shall have petting *ad nauseam*," and she held out her hand to him; "only do not make too much clever talk, or you will annihilate poor little me altogether."

He bowed over her hand and kissed it with the tears in his eyes. The lonely man was touched by this mark of womanly regard.

"So you are going to start an educational newspaper, you say, and for women, too! I am afraid we are progressing too fast. I should like to creep back into the last century," she said, leading him away from the sentimental and putting him back on his pet hobby-horse again. "It is all no good, my dear man, I feel quite sure of it. Fools will be fools still, whatever newspapers you may write or schools you may institute. I for one would never either read the one or go to the other."

"And yet you appreciate talent."

"Ah! but I should not if it were very common. Then I should want a fool to exhibit at my parties, as the kings had jesters of old."

"Even nonsense requires more teaching than you suspect," he replied, laughing. "To be amusing it must be sparkling, to be sparkling it must have its source from the fount of knowledge; and a man who talks nonsense professionally is indeed a dreary individual, unless he have a flash or two of genius about him."

" Oh ! if you are going to analyse every-thing, even nonsense, pray spare me, and tell me what you want women to do and to be, when they have received all this highly intellectual teaching ; not helpmeets for man, —for if they take it all in they will be in-comparably superior to him."

" I hope not, if the same amount of pres-sure is applied to both sexes. But the main object, I take it, of the higher education of women is to make them more self-reliant than they now are, more capable of contribut-ing to their support, and finding for them-selves avocations in which their talents may be employed and their purses filled. To women of the middle classes I most particu-larly allude."

" Poor wretches,—well, if a woman can-not find a man to work for her she must be a poor thing, with all her learning. I am a fool, as I have previously told you, therefore my opinion is not worth much, but I strongly suspect you men are carving out misery for the next generation by putting everything and everybody in the wrong place. The mental training from which you expect so much is sure to fall short of its adjudged mark, self-sufficiency and arrogance will assert themselves in its place ; and you men will find out when too late that the pretty little dolls, who are contented to be coaxed and played with, are far preferable to these overpowering young women who are ready to crush you with an avalanche of big words at every turn."

" This is viewing the leading question of the day from a very low standard."

" Taken at a silly woman's focus,—so be it,—but, nevertheless, you will never make me think otherwise than that the system will prove homicidal. This is surely not the sort of opening you meditate for Pettita, that she is to be crammed with learning and made horrid and disagreeable ? "

" Something must be done for those girls,"

answered Mr. Griesnach gravely, "their income is totally inadequate to meet their requirements as gentlewomen."

"Well, bring high pressure to bear on Margaret if you like, but do leave Pettita alone. I cannot and will not have her spoiled, which is sure to happen the moment she is taught."

"But, my dear Mrs. Leigh, Pettita is a girl with strong latent ambitions; her yearnings and longings for a world beyond her own little one are already developing themselves."

"And do you think women never had yearnings and longings, as you call them, before this higher education system was the general topic? It is no use to talk to me; I do not see the good of it and I never shall. Let us take Pettita, for instance —put her in a hotbed and force her brain to its utmost, — what is the result, the money-making return you expect from all this?"

"A highly educated woman must find a

value for her talents?" answered Mr. Griesnach.

"So I should imagine—by going out as a
daily governess and leading a life of drudgery.
It might suit Margaret, it shall not be tried
for Pettita.   Women are of a totally different
organisation to men.   Take an ignorant
woman's word for it, my dear Mr. Griesnach, one who knows the sex much better
than you can possibly do; it is useless
trying to drench us with the heavy knowledge you give to boys, in nine cases out of
ten it produces nothing but self-sufficiency
and impertinence; we frequently have one
leading talent, which, if properly worked,
will bear fruit, and failing that, which only
developes itself in the favoured few, we are
far better left to our housewifely duties, our
frivolities and our gossip, as the case
may be."

"You do not draw a very flattering picture
of your sex," he said, smiling.

"Do not misunderstand, I think my own
sex in its way quite the equal of yours, it is

brighter, lighter, more brilliant; but the very qualities we have which lend their radiance to you, and which tend to gladden many an overworked man's leisure hours, you men are yourselves labouring to extinguish, and are trying to taint us with the attributes of that most unpleasant of all mortals, a learned don. All I can say is, I fervently hope that you will never succeed, or if you do, that you will be made to suffer for it."

" Do you then altogether object to a woman making any mark for herself in public life ? "

" Not a bit. Prudery is not one of my tenets, but I object to her standing on platforms haranguing about things entirely out of her province, and trying to take fresh responsibilities and troubles upon herself when it seems to me she has quite enough without them. Defend me from a strong-minded woman, but then you know I am a fool, and that may account to a great extent for my antipathy. I believe the whole thing is got up by a faction for the sake of notoriety, but as notoriety pays better perhaps than celebrity, *Vive* the 'Educational Argus.'"

"Pardon me, Mrs. Leigh, but this is a harsh judgment even from a woman," exclaimed Mr. Griesnach, half-laughing, half prepared to be affronted, "you do not surely imagine that I would lend myself to a mere money-making scheme in which my opinions did not fully concur."

"Oh! then you really believe in the advantages to accrue from this revolution in the old state of things; now tell me what they are, I am willing to be converted, if possible."

" Extended education ought most emphatically to be an object, because by it alone can the interests and position of women be improved, and even you will, I fancy, admit that there are grounds. Every year in this country an increasing number of women are left to struggle for themselves in life, their instruction seems to me then to have become of immense commercial value."

" But the market is over-stocked," cried
Mrs. Leigh, " and teach them as much as
you will, there is no work left for them to
do when they are taught, consequently they
would be much happier knowing less. Now,
Mr. Griesnach, we have before us two living
instances of moneyless girls wanting work
and an opening, so all these fine theories can
very readily be put into practice. What are
you going to do with them? Pettita says
she is going on the stage."

" Heaven forbid ! " he exclaimed, but Mrs.
Leigh burst out laughing.

" Why, you are as absurd as Margaret, do
you mean to say the girl will not be much
happier following the bent of her own in-
clinations than being forced into work for
which she has no taste or talent? I feel sure
Bohemia is a very pleasant country."

He shook his head gravely.

" You have never tried it, and therefore
scarcely know the horrors which counter-
balance its seeming charms. This then is
Pettita's view for her future career," he con-

tinued, as though half talking to himself,
"foolish child, foolish child ; she never told
me though ; but it must be stopped, it must
be stopped."

"You bigot," cried Mrs. Leigh, still
laughing, "you call yourself an advocate for
women's work, and then when a young thing
presents herself with a developing talent,
you cry out crush it back, crush it back, it
is the wrong one, we want another."

"Margaret will never consent," he per-
sisted ; "think of their position as gentlewomen."

"Position ! fiddle-de-dee, that is a word
that will be obsolete in the next generation ;
the 'pinnacled aristocracy' has only a few
old-fashioned champions, like Lady Bluntisfield, left even now ; these levelling days do
not admit of many class distinctions. Now
answer me honestly, Mr. Griesnach, would
not you rather that Pettita were an *artiste*
than a governess."

"If she were a successful *artiste*, yes,
perhaps."

"And who says she is not going to be successful? She must take her chance in that like other things."

Mr. Griesnach did not speak again for two or three minutes,—he was thinking; at last he burst out with,

"It is a fearful trial, though, to see the child you would watch over and keep from harm, exposed to the buffets, cuffs, and libels of a bitter world."

"Or the applause, admiration, and laudation of a delighted audience; every picture has its reverse side, every phase in life its temptations."

"But the stage for Pettita," he went on.

"Her mother," said Mrs. Leigh quietly.

He started up.

"Was a *danseuse*, yes, but the girls do not know it; never let them be told; how did you find it out?"

Mrs. Leigh smiled complacently.

"I know most things," she observed.

The fact was, she knew nothing of the matter, only a vague suspicion had on more than one occasion crossed her mind that the penniless Lima beauty might have a history, so she threw out a little hook, the fish nibbled, and the required information was caught.

" And with this knowledge," she went on talking quietly, " is it surprising that Pettita should have a taste for the foot-lights."

But Mr. Griesnach was beyond listening patiently, he was shambling about the room in his awkward disjointed way, groaning and muttering, and seemingly regardless of Mrs. Leigh's presence. Bertha rose, and walking up to him in her noiseless fashion led him gently back to his arm-chair by the fire.

" I cannot allow you to excite yourself thus, indeed it is not good for you, you will be quite ill, and your health, in my eyes at all events, is far more important than that foolish girl's caprices."

" The first moment I saw her I knew she resembled her mother," he went on.

" Well, never mind that now, do be calm

and reasonable. I am going to write to Pettita to come to town, and then you shall talk to her, and I will talk to her, and between us we will see whether a ⌐middle course cannot be arranged. I have my little projects."

"My dear lady, I have been at my wits' end to know what to do for those girls ever since I became aware of their forlorn, almost penniless condition."

"Well, never mind, they will fall on their feet never fear. You go on with your 'Educational Argus' (I dare say it will prove a very useful organ), and your newspaper articles; do not roll yourself up in morbid thoughts and neglect them, there is nothing like having a hold on the press when you have anything to push."

"Ah!" he said, rising to take his leave, "I suspect you know far more of the workings of things in general than in the early part of our conversation you would have led me to believe."

"Mere instinct, my friend, and that

quick-sightedness in which we so far surpass you men, and of which you would rob us when you would dull our natural capacities by too much learning."

Mr. Griesnach, however, was too much taken up by his thoughts about Pettita's future to feel disposed for farther argument, thus Mrs. Leigh carried her love of excessive womanliness to the end of the discussion by having the last word—and so they parted.

She threw herself back on her sofa to rest for awhile after the somewhat fatiguing conversations and combinations of the day.

CHAPTER VIII.

IN LONDON.

" You do not mean to say that this is London and that I am really and truly here at last? It is much smokier and dingier than the country, but never mind that. Oh! it is too delightful. How good of you to invite me, you sweet old dear!" and Pettita, but a few hours since arrived from Woodlands, danced about the little drawing-room in Belgrave Street, in a perfect ecstasy of delight; "and 'old Dick' is coming to dinner you say, Mrs. Leigh; by the by, Madge says I am not to call him 'old Dick,' but I cannot help it, it comes naturally."

" ' Old Dick ' is going to have you taught,

he is editing a newspaper on purpose, he wants to bring you out as a philosopheress, a sort of she-Hegel or Comte in petticoats."

"Good gracious, how alarming! but of course you are only poking fun at me."

"Not a bit of it, the idea of the footlights frightens him excessively, so he means to have you crammed with learning till you have passed your examination in all sorts of 'ologies,' and, with a pair of very ill-shaped spectacles on your nose, are fit to stand on a platform from whence you will be expected to harangue a very large audience of the unenlightened masses."

"What fun it would be!" cried the girl, "just to do it for once, if one could only get the 'ologies' into one's head without learning them."

Mrs. Leigh put on a serio-comic face.

"My dear Pettita, I am surprised to hear you talk in this flippant strain. Are you not aware, young woman, that you have come to London to work, and that therefore you must put aside all frivolity and levity, and must devote yourself with a will to the pursuit of knowledge? You will hear of nothing else in this great capital, we have all gone mad on the subject of education; in fact, Bedlam is so full of educational monomaniacs that they are thinking of building another hospital."

Pettita sat down on a low stool on the hearthrug looking very dismal, almost as though she were going to cry.

"And is it really true?" she asked, "that there is nothing for me to do in London unless I go to school again? And I do so hate all books except just those that it pleases my fancy to read; I don't want to be taught grammar and geometry, and astronomy and political economy. I abominate them all, they are only fit for boys."

"It shall not if it does not like," said Mrs. Leigh, leaning over her and smoothing her hair; "it shall marry a rich husband, and he shall have learnt all the objectionable things."

"I don't want a rich husband; I want to do something for myself without going to school again at eighteen," and Pettita pushed Mrs. Leigh off somewhat roughly, in her petted way.

"Well, my dear child, if you will neither accept the new-fashioned system nor the old one, what is to be done?"

"I won't be fettered," cried Pettita, jumping up. "I will neither be tied to old folios nor to a man for his money-bags. Let us go to the theatre to-night, dear Mrs. Leigh; I am sure that is the only life that will suit me. I must have glitter and admiration, and light and a brilliant career, or I shall die of starvation."

"Oh! you poor little Lima offshoot; and this is the girl they want to turn into a bit of dried parchment. We cannot go to the theatre to-night, darling, because Mr. Griesnach is coming, but some night soon you shall see the very best play in London."

Pettita began to pirouette about the room with a sort of baby glee.

Mrs. Leigh watched her and made her mental comments. Bertha was a keen observer of character, or she would not have succeeded so well in her various little plans and intrigues. She smiled quietly to herself as she regarded Pettita from under her long lashes.

"There is not much of the stuff strong-minded women are made of in her composition," she thought to herself. "Fancy trying to teach her; nothing would ever make her understand the meaning of the word 'value,' and without that you would not make much impression."

"Glitter and warmth and brightness, so that is what you want, Pettita," she said at last, finishing her comments out loud, "and no work? I am sorry there are so many like you, child."

"Oh! I will work, Mrs. Leigh, but not at books. I will dance or act or sing all day and all night if it will only pay Madge's bills."

"Can you sing?" asked Mrs. Leigh,

who felt that if she had a voice worth
training perhaps the Gordian knot might be
untied.

Pettita began to carol like a bird as she
went on with her graceful dance about the
room. Mrs. Leigh, ensconced among her
sofa cushions, looked on and listened; she
was searching for the one talent, which, a
few days previously, she had assured Mr.
Griesnach was to be found in every woman
who was above par; and this she hoped
and believed Pettita to be. Generally
bright and clever, there was no doubt the
girl was; 'accomplished' was the young
lady's term by which she would have been
designated had money allowed her to
dawdle along the path of life in which
she was born. The object, however, now
was to find the accomplishment which
would bear forcing. She had never had
any teachers but her father and Margaret;
thus learning with her had been very desultory, and talent had been left a good
deal to its natural growth. Margaret's

somewhat dry, matter-of-fact view of study was but little in accordance with Pettita's more vivacious and impressionable temperament. The books she would read with avidity Margaret generally disapproved ; and had it not been that Captain St. Orme spoiled his youngest born and let her do exactly as she liked, they would probably have been taken away altogether.

Left to their own luxuriant growth, her talents then had undergone but little pruning and cutting, except occasionally, when Margaret managed to get her incisive scissors among the branches ; but this was so seldom, and raised such a storm of rebellion when it did happen, that the advantages derived were but small. Thus, training to be commenced at eighteen was scarcely likely to prove very effectual, and well might her friends look at each other and ask, "What is to be done with Pettita ?"

Mrs. Leigh sat and watched the girl's mad frolics about the room, and did not speak for some little time,—she was con-

sidering. She was desirous, after her fashion,
to do something substantial for her *protégée*.
She was not altogether ill-natured and un-
benevolent; it was only when any one got
in her way that Bertha Leigh would scheme
and intrigue till she annoyed, or perhaps
crushed, them. For the present, at all
events, Pettita was in high favour, and
Bertha was really intent on doing her the
best turn she could, according to the focus
from which she viewed her case. Be
it remembered, Mrs. Leigh generally made
her own lens, and to any one but herself they
would have been very misty, darkness and
general vagueness would have oppressed the
uninitiated, but then, of course, they could
know nothing of the conjuror's tricks by
which Bertha filled in roseate hues and
golden tints. She was very capable of
taking care of herself, no one more so; but
was she a safe and sure guide for a young,
highly imaginative, impressionable girl like
Pettita St. Orme? That was the question
those who knew her well would assuredly have

asked. At last Pettita, tired by her somewhat childish gambols, came and sat down
on the sofa beside her friend and patroness.
In a moment Bertha's arm was round her,
and she was drawn lovingly towards her.

"Poor little thing," she said compassionately, "I am so sorry you feel obliged
to work ; you might amuse yourself so pleasantly if you only had money."

"Don't pity me, pray don't pity me,"
cried Pettita, flushing and starting back;
"money is pleasant I make no doubt, at
least I know that poverty is utterly miserable. To see Madge pinching and striving
and slaving to make two ends which are ever
so far apart meet, is a dreary picture to
have constantly before one's eyes, and to tell
the truth, I cannot stand it much longer,
though I know she draws a curtain over the
half of it, poor dear; but I will not
be pitied. I want to know whether you
think I am any good, whether the stage will
have me, in fact."

"Oh! yes, the stage will have you, I

make no doubt," answered Mrs. Leigh, looking straight before her, and speaking in her
low quiet way, "but have you considered
all you will have to contend against before
you get there—Margaret's tears, Mr. Griesnach's frowns, and when the first have been
dried up and the puckers smoothed out of
the second, then there is the training;—you
must learn your business, my child."

Pettita looked very demure.

"Learning, always learning, Mrs. Leigh;
can nothing be done without learning? And
I thought I was to become great and rich
all at once."

At that moment the door opened, and
Mr. Griesnach was announced; he was early,
earlier by half an hour than he had been
expected, but he was impatient to see
Pettita. Mrs. Leigh glanced at the clock
on the mantelpiece, this unpunctuality was
an infringement on the laws of society
which did not please her, and might, she
thought, have proved very inconvenient. A
fidgety, irritable temperament was a phase

of human nature with which personally she was wholly unacquainted, though it might prove amusing as a psychological study, always provided that its vagaries and eccentricities were not allowed to interfere with her arrangements and plans.

She only smiled, however, when Mr. Griesnach excused himself for his over-impatience, and then took up the thread of the conversation by telling him that Pettita had evidently more than believed the old saying that London streets were paved with gold, for she anticipated that glory was to be met at every turn, but she added,

" *We* know, dear Mr. Griesnach, do we not, that the road to Fame is up-hill, and that it is only notoriety that is easily attained ? "

" ' Genius never fails to be accompanied by a martyr's crown,' as said the great Goethe*," he replied softly, looking sadly on the girl as he spoke.

* Wo du das Genie erblickst
  Erblickst du auch zugleich die Marterkrone.

He knew full well that the life she in her youthful enthusiasm imagined would be fraught with so much happiness, would probably prove a disappointment and a blank, at best a fret and a perpetual torment. Who has cast himself into the troubled waters of public life, into whichever of its many streamlets his proclivities may have led him, and has not found it so? How many a man, to-day vested with almost god-like attributes, is to-morrow cast forth naked to be scourged, while the *vox populi*, but yesterday so loud in praise, finds no epithets too foul to lavish on the fallen idol? and, as Mrs. Leigh had justly observed, to reach that unsafe pinnacle was no easy road. Dangers, vexations, rebuffs, beset the aspirant for Fame at every turn; how many young hearts are broken in the fight, how few minds have the strength to pursue the world-weary pilgrimage to its end! All this and more did Richard Griesnach know full well as he stood and looked at Pettita. What man interested in a woman's welfare would choose such a lot for her ? Yet what was to be done ? Of money she had little, of contentment she had none. The restlessness of her nature demanded employment ; the good that was in her made her long to do what was possible towards paying those dreadful bills which were always worrying Margaret.

" Women's work ; " the words are passed from tongue to tongue, the subject is discussed largely in all its bearings. Yet no one seemed able to decide how Pettita's efforts were to be directed, there seemed nothing she could do, no portal open to her. 'The fault was entirely her own,' is the impatient answer. To a certain extent true. She is a very woman, impressionable, illogical, led by instinct rather than reason, fond of admiration, pliable and loving, made wretched by a cross word, won over by a kind one. With all these attributes, totally unfit to struggle along a hard road, and yet, poor child, no other seemed likely to present itself. From the stage, at any cost,

Richard Griesnach had determined she should be saved ; he had been thinking the matter over carefully and painfully since he was last at Mrs. Leigh's, and had resolved to do his utmost to prevent it.

She sat for some few minutes looking very subdued, a tear-drop glistening in each eye, then she dashed them away and started up full of hope and life once more.

"I can dance," she cried, "and I have read in books that people are paid for dancing; if you think I am too great a fool ever to be famous, at least let me get money and help Madge."

Mrs. Leigh glanced at Mr. Griesnach and smiled, but he turned away with a shudder.

"My child," he said in a low voice, " you know nothing of life, or you would not talk at random thus."

"You all find fault," cried Pettita pettishly, "but no one suggests a career, so there is nothing left but to take the law in my own hands and make one for myself. I hate this perpetual ' don't do this ' and ' you must not do the other,' so I shall end by doing as I like."

"Anything but the stage," broke in Mr. Griesnach, his words coming out in a half-choked way.

"I thought you admired the drama," she cried; "why, I am sure it was entirely owing to your talking so much one day at Wood-lands about 'legitimate drama' that I rummaged out a lot of old books and devoured Beaumont and Fletcher and Massinger till Margaret took them all away."

"The drama, yes, one bows before intellect,—but to dance! My God, Pettita, I feel almost mad at the very thought."

Mrs. Leigh, who had witnessed Mr. Griesnach's excitement on a previous occasion and did not wish for a repetition, now interrupted them, speaking with her flute-like voice.

"Do let us be happy to-night, and not get into any uncomfortable discussions; a very old friend of mine, who knows more of the stage than we can possibly do, for she has

been before the public for the last forty
years, shall come and have a talk to the
child here, and we will more or less abide
by her *dictum*; now, to please me, say no
more about it for this one evening. Arguing
before dinner is very bad for the digestion,
and poor dear Mr. Griesnach looks quite
weary and ill. We are going to devote ourselves to petting him, are we not, Pettita."

Soon the dinner was announced, and as
Bertha aptly turned the conversation whenever it touched on dangerous ground, the
time passed pleasantly enough. Any one
who knew Bertha Leigh well would inevitably have discovered that she was bored;
she yawned occasionally in a suppressed sort
of way, and was very *distraite* when not
absolutely called upon to speak. Perhaps she
was wondering why she had entangled herself in this new mesh, and troubled herself
about the affairs of people who were after
all nothing to her. One thing is very
certain, that she was deciding in her own
mind that Richard Griesnach should not be

a too-frequent visitor in Belgrave Street.
" Would it not be possible," she thought,
" to bring about a marriage between him and
Margaret ? That might afford her a little
amusing occupation, she must see if it
could not be accomplished."

CHAPTER IX.

A REVELATION.

PETTITA had been gone some days, and Margaret was alone in the cottage. Alone with her perplexities, her troubles, her unpaid bills. She was glad Pettita was gone, though she sorely missed her vivacity and her prattle; still it was more or less of a relief to her overstrained nerves to feel that there was no occasion to hide her annoyances and anxieties under a cheerful smile, that she might lay her poor tired aching head on the table beside those endless account-books without being questioned as to her weariness and depression. No one but Margaret herself knew how strenuously she had hitherto fought to save Pettita's young life from being enveloped in the sort of cloud which hung over her own.

Now as she sits in the little drawing-room everything round her looks very confused and out of place, for Margaret has been having a general rummage over old letters and papers, and she has at length sunk down tired out and haunted by the old memories, which have been one after another awakened during her search. Margaret was by no means of a dreamy temperament, she was active and practical ; if those money difficulties had not well-nigh crushed her with their weight, she would have been ever cheerful and busy in her placid, undemonstrative way, but she so frequently knew not what to do, or which way to turn for the best, that she had of late taken to sitting with her hands in her lap puzzling her poor young brain over the future till it was well-nigh worn out. These old letters, too, with their many sad recollections had not helped to cheer her, reminding her as they did how thoroughly she was alone in the world, with no one to shield her from trouble, and a young sister dependent on her for counsel and protection. Presently she thought she heard some one at the outer door, and she started to her feet and began to arrange her papers vigorously; the Squire was almost her only visitor, and, with the pride inherent in her nature, she did not wish him to find her dejected and out of sorts with herself. It was not, however, his big jovial voice which called to Margaret as the drawing-room door opened, nor his benevolent face which met hers as she turned round anxiously. It was Richard Griesnach, pale, haggard, and with an excited feverish look in his eyes, who walked nervously up to her.

" Pettita,—my sister," she asked in a low voice, as though fright rendered her almost powerless, " she is not ill? Oh! Mr. Griesnach, tell me the worst at once, what has brought you here ?"

" Pettita is quite well. I did not mean

to frighten you," he said hurriedly, "I only came down for an hour or two to talk over affairs. You and I, Margaret, can settle things better without the child."

She gave a sigh of relief, and then in her quiet, thoughtful way, wheeled him a cosy chair, and suggested that he should have some luncheon before they began to discuss business. But Richard Griesnach seemed restless and irritable. Notwithstanding his assurance that nothing was wrong, it was obvious that he had not come to Woodlands simply in a calm spirit for a practical talk over affairs with Margaret. Yet he said nothing to the point, but talked in a random way about a diversity of subjects, while she busied herself over his creature comforts. The litter of papers all about the room did not seem to please him, and he testily asked Margaret why she had not burned them all without looking at them. A suggestion which seemed to amuse the practical Margaret, as she wondered to herself whether he were likely to prove the adviser she had hoped if that were his mode of conducting business. He looked at her unruffled face, and concluded that she had found no secrets which he would fain conceal from her.

"Your father's desk," he asked, "have you opened it?"

"Not yet; but I suppose it must be done. I cannot do otherwise than hold it sacred, and have sometimes thought of putting it away untouched."

"Have you sufficient confidence in me, Margaret, to let me have it just as it is? You may trust me to bring you any paper relating either to your own or Pettita's welfare."

Margaret regarded him with some surprise, but she believed in him fully, and when a woman believes what will she not entrust to a man?

"You shall have it willingly," she answered. "I am very sure poor dear papa would have wished it; how good of you, Mr. Griesnach, to try and save me from pain!"

"Try and save you from pain? Ay, would I, but I fear there is pain in store for both of us if we do not strengthfully face the danger and avert it. Do you know that Pettita is bent on going on the stage?"

Margaret started as though a knife had suddenly pierced her flesh.

"I have heard of this before," she said in a low voice, "but had hoped it was mere childish talk. Do you think Mrs. Leigh is urging her on?"

Mr. Griesnach looked up inquiringly, but the scales had not yet fallen from his eyes, and to his blinded vision all Bertha Leigh's shortcomings were perfections.

"No, certainly not; she is very rational and sensible about it."

"What is to be done, what can be done?" asked Margaret piteously; "it is too dreadful to contemplate."

"Reason must, if possible, be brought into the balance," he answered somewhat sternly. "Look you, my dear young lady, some time ago you and I agreed to differ on

the subject of women's work; now, mark
you, I have not the same horror of the stage
even for Pettita which you profess; if I saw
or thought she was likely to make her mark
as a great actress, I should yield at once,
but I do not, she will never rise above
——" what her mother was before her he
had nearly said, but he stopped himself in
time and turned away with a half sob.

Margaret rose and began hurriedly to put
the papers back in the drawers from whence
she had taken them.

" What are you doing?" he asked at last,
after there had been a long silence.

"I am coming back to town with you,"
she said. "I ought never to have left the
child, even for a moment, something tells
me utterly and thoroughly to distrust Mrs.
Leigh."

"You are right to watch over your
sister, but, as for your distrust of Mrs.
Leigh, that I feel sure is a mere woman's
caprice. Pettita could scarcely have found
a better friend, or be received in a house

where she would find pleasanter or more agreeable society."

Margaret looked up at him as she stopped for a moment in her work of cramming the papers back still unsorted into the drawers of a davenport.

"Pleasant society and pauperism will never amalgamate," she said coldly; "and if Pettita is only to obtain pleasant society at the risk of losing her position as her father's daughter, I sincerely wish Mrs. Leigh had never come to Woodlands to tempt her. She would have been happy enough here, if she had not had glimpses into a world so different from what her own can ever be."

" You are wrong," he said; " your sister's warm impulsive nature could not have been satisfied long with the 'still life' you would accept gratefully. Be thankful then that she has found a friend in Mrs. Leigh."

"She *is* impulsive and frequently discontented with what she calls 'monotony,'" murmured Margaret musingly, half talking to herself. " I wonder why she has a character so unlike the family type; all the St. Ormes were cold and calm and proud. Pettita, poor child, seems to possess no pride at all."

Mr. Griesnach looked at Margaret as she went on reasoning in a quiet unruffled way. " Was it all St. Orme blood that flowed in their veins?" he would have asked, but he rose from his seat, walked to the window, and looked out ; he knew full well the severe stab Margaret's proud nature had yet to receive when she learnt the history of her mother's early life, and had her faith shaken in that 'pride of race' with which she believed her father and all the St. Ormes to have been so strongly imbued. The papers were, at last, out of sight, and the room was restored by Margaret's busy hands to its usual state of tidy formalism. Then she stood for a minute or two and looked into the fire, as though she would find a plan for future action in the changing coals. Mr. Griesnach, with his back to her, was still studying the dreary, leafless winter landscape. Both had much upon their minds, neither quite knew how to shape it into words.

" Let us go," said Margaret at last. " I shall bring Pettita back with me here till March, and then if she still wishes to return to London, I will take a small lodging where she must be content to live quietly; we cannot afford more, and as gentlewomen belonging to an old family how can we work?"

Pettita's voice was wanting, or the cry would have been, " Madge, I am no longer a baby, and *will* only do as I like," but Mr. Griesnach heard the echo in the distance.

" Again, you forget the difference in your temperaments," he said, as he walked up to where Margaret was standing.

" Nonsense," she ·answered, the family decision coming out strongly when she thought herself thwarted, " she is only a child, and must be made to obey ; she knows nothing of life,—how can she judge for herself? I really believe, Mr. Griesnach, that you would listen to her whims till you attended to them."

He bowed his head down on his breast.

"If I thought she cared or could ever care for me, how gladly would I protect and shelter her!" he said gravely. "Of money I have little to offer her, but enough I hope to keep her above want."

Margaret gave a little start of astonishment, and then looked at him without speaking, a very appalled expression on her face the while. She in her turn heard the echo of Pettita's young voice laughing over 'Old Dick' and his peculiarities. And as the picture of her joyous impetuous sister in all the freshness of her developing beauty rose before her mind, and she contrasted it with the feeble flickering blighted life of the man who stood beside her, she almost cried out impulsively, "I know Pettita's character after all better than you do, for I know she will never be persuaded to do this thing." An instinctive dread of wounding him, however, tied her tongue and she only murmured softly after awhile,

"You are good, too good. Time alone can solve the mysteries of the future."

"Then you think I have no hope?" he asked eagerly, looking suddenly up at her with those fiery little eyes.

"I cannot say, I am quite ignorant on the subject. You have taken me so by surprise, I am quite incapable of forming an opinion. Pettita is very young,—can never yet have thought of either love or marriage."

"But do you think she likes me?" he asked with a *naïveté* which showed how a strong emotion may bring a great intellect down almost to the level of a child's capacity.

"Oh! yes, she likes you, of that I am very sure," she answered shortly. "Did she hate you, you would have more chance," she might have added. Strong love not unfrequently springs from hatred,—never from mere liking.

"And may I not hope for countenance and

help from you?" he asked, seizing her nervously by the wrist.

"Have you not told me yourself that Pettita is somewhat impatient of control? Words from me would have but little weight if your wooing prove ineffectual."

For Margaret, although she reverenced Richard Griesnach as an intellectual sensible man who had been her father's dearest friend, was scarcely prepared to accept him as a husband for her bright young sister.

"I have not spoken to her on the subject. She knows nothing of my feelings," he said hurriedly. "I wished first to talk to you, to learn if you thought I had any hope, but I see in your eyes that it is all vain, the curse of my deformity will blight my life even to its end, and no bright eyes fraught with love shall ever pierce my gloom."

And he dropped into the nearest chair, and hid his face as though he would not have Margaret gaze upon its agony. Margaret was not like Bertha Leigh, she could be practically kind and hospitable, but she was almost powerless to deal with a strong emotion. She stood and looked at Richard Griesnach, her heart full of regretful annoyance at the turn events had taken, but for some time no words rose to her lips. How often does it happen that those who feel the most keenly for the griefs and vexations of others, find the fewest words to express themselves, and therefore how generally misunderstood they are in this world of ours!

As it was, Richard Griesnach was the first to break the silence. He looked up at Margaret and saw the tear-drops glistening in the sorrowful eyes which bent so compassionately on him.

"You cannot help it, child," he said, striving to smile. "Do not let sorrow for me be added to the list of your troubles, which God knows is a long one. Let us try to be tough, Margaret, and make the best of life. Whatever comes, my first thoughts will ever be centred in Pettita; do not fear that I shall desert her because she cannot love a blighted old fellow like me,—how should she, poor child? I was mad to hope it."

"Oh! Mr. Griesnach, please do not talk so bitterly, we neither of us know what Pettita's feelings towards you may be."

In her woman's fear of wounding him she threw him this straw, though in her heart she believed it to be a broken one; he seized it, however, like a drowning man, and a bright light for a moment illumined the intelligent face that was so frequently darkened by shadows.

"We do not know, true we none of us know,—if the future had not hope to lead us on, it would indeed be a dreary barren waste;" and then he sank back again in his chair as though to dwell on the new train of thoughts which had suggested themselves.

"Shall we not start for London?" asked Margaret; her practical mind was dwelling on the fact that she wanted if possible to bring Pettita back to Woodlands at once, that the short winter day was waning fast, and that on reaching the metropolis, where she would be very strange, she had to find a night's lodging for herself.

"Ay, of course," he answered, rising. "I am forgetting everything in my selfishness, we will go certainly, but I doubt much if the child will return with you, Margaret. 'Forward, ho!' is her motto I strongly suspect."

Margaret's brow contracted somewhat, and her lips became compressed, she did not understand the word "Disobedience," and according to her views Pettita was in duty bound to listen to the elder sister, who was her sole surviving relation.

So some half hour later, leaving the cottage in charge of the solitary servant who composed the St. Orme's establishment, Mr. Griesnach and Margaret started for the station, which, by taking a short cut across some fields, was but about ten minutes' walk from Woodlands. Somewhat to Margaret's astonishment, even the excitement under which he laboured did not allow Richard Griesnach to forget the desk, which fortunately was not a large one, or it would have been scarcely possible for the little man to have carried it so persistently as he did, refusing every offer from Margaret to relieve him, if only for a few moments, from its weight.

CHAPTER X.

SHYLOCK AND JESSICA IN THE NINETEENTH CENTURY.

A DIRTY street in the immediate neighbourhood of Oxford Street,—costermongers' barrows laden with the refuse of the markets passing continually up and down, while their owners call your attention to the cheapness of their contents in clamorous chorus inharmoniously blended with the grating and jingling of barrel-organs and hurdy-gurdys, —on a hot day not unfrequently redolent of that fragrance for which, according to Coleridge, Cologne is so renowned. Beauty? No, there is little enough of that, poverty is rarely beautiful if you look at it closely,

M

though artists tell you that there is a certain amount of picturesqueness about a dirty child with coal black eyes and luscious blood-red lips,—but the illusion soon vanishes. Take up your dainty skirts as you pass down this particular street, and hold them as high as modesty will permit when you stand on the doorstep of the dilapidated dingy looking old abode into which we mean to have a peep. Paint and whitewash cost money, and the owner of that particular house is not lavish in his expenditure ; perhaps he is one of those benighted individuals who believe in the picturesqueness of dirt. If you ask the neighbours about him, they will tell you with a shrug that he is a Jew, and so he is, but he has his good points for all that. He has some of the eccentricities which are usually ascribed to the great Jewish family, but he is not without much of the large-heartedness and benevolence which Christians are so backward in allowing to them; yet he is a Jew, a very Jew, a bigot to the faith of his fathers.

Well, as the unoiled street-door creaks back on its hinges you start and feel for your scented handkerchief, for a smell of dust and general fustiness seems to get into your throat; but be brave and go on,—if you do carry off an occasional cobweb, it will hurt the spiders more than it will you. The journey onwards is fraught with difficulty, you say, and no wonder, for the house is piled with works of art from the garret to the cellar, not artistically arranged to please the eye of *cognoscenti*, but crowded together so as to occupy the least possible space. Pause a moment on the first landing, there is a little gleam of sunshine dancing in through that high window; look at that blackwood cabinet of Italian work with its lapis-lazuli panels, at that bronze statue of Venus, and then above your head at the rare oriental lamp with its quaint Arabian characters and enamels rich in gorgeous colouring. If you cannot appreciate these, if you are only one of those senseless automata who exclaim "How pretty" when

you behold a work of art unparalleled
among the riches of kingdoms, then turn
back and do not profane the old Jew's den
by your presence, for there they all are
those priceless emanations from the hands
and brains of genius. " He buys them and
sells them that he may become rich," perhaps you observe sneeringly. Ay, but he
regards them and handles them with love,
they are his children, part of his very life,—
with one glance he can distinguish the
spurious from the real.

The lower or dining rooms have been
turned into a sort of warehouse, where the
more cumbersome but less precious of this
wonderful collection of art-treasures are
kept locked ; it is therefore on the first floor
that the old Jew may be found, seated at a
small ormolu table in the corner of the front
room, deeply engrossed adding up long lines
of figures, while some of the loveliest gems
to be found in the kingdom of art are
scattered pell-mell all around him. He is
himself a quaint looking old specimen of

God's workmanship. Small in limb and feature, he is bent nearly double from age, and his tiny white hands tremble with emotion as he touches some pet treasure; altogether he looks a very fragile and decrepit little old man as he sits there, his white hair hanging lankily and scantily about his neck from beneath his velvet cap. It is not till he looks up at you with his keen hawk-like eyes that you discover that the flame is not entirely extinguished in the nearly spent body, and from the energy, passion, and resolution still lurking in those little balls of fire you seem to form an instanta-neous retrospect of the life that is hidden behind the veil of years. He is urbane and courteous in his manners too, though a fine ear may detect a vein of sarcasm which never forsakes his conversation, the result probably of his cosmopolitanism, for intimate knowledge of humanity in some of its coarsest forms, as he had experienced it, had hardened him, while it had called forth a power of latent satire in his nature.

Although he had lived in England so long as to be almost naturalised, yet it was not his birthplace, nor had the language ever become wholly familiar to him. No one knew where he was born, 'Am Rhein' was the only answer an interrogatory on the subject ever called forth,—verily he could not deny his Vaterland even-had he been so disposed, for the hard guttural German accents would intermingle with his English talk.

But while we have been describing so far the interior of the old Jew's abode, the sun's rays, which for a few moments commingled their beauty with the rich colourings of art, have died away behind the chimney-pots and sombre-looking houses which the English love, and old Jacobsen's tremulous fingers are rolling up his papers with care.

" Good ; ja, so far it is good," and there is a faint smile of pleasure on his pale seamed face as, having finished his work, he lies back in his chair.

In a few minutes, in the increasing darkness, you can see nothing but those bright glowing little eyes which seem to light up the corner with their brilliancy.

" Ah ! but wherefore then comes the child not," he exclaimed at length, " is it possible that absorbed in my calculations I forget her ? "

" I am here, my father, " said a young voice from the doorway, though no one could be seen, " but why are you sitting there without a light ? It is so wretched to be in the dark. I am afraid to come in for fear of creating a misfortune."

" No, child, make no trial, I will come to you, but wherefore you seem so still, are you fatigued, my daughter ? "

" Yes, very tired," she answered somewhat wearily, "but no matter, come up in my room, father, it is bright and cosy there, this gloom gives me the shivers, there is a little supper too quite ready."

The old man groped his way to the door without any difficulty and followed his daughter up the stairs, of which with the

elastic step of youth she had already gained
the top. Through the open door of the
front room a bright light shone, revealing
one habitable spot in this otherwise
wretchedly comfortless abode. The girl
looked up at him as he entered, then she
turned her face suddenly away as though
she feared to betray an emotion under which
she was labouring. Something had evidently
occurred to disturb her, for she was usually
calm and self-possessed enough. Mimi
Jacobsen was not exactly beautiful, her
features were of too stern a type, but she
was picturesque and regal looking. She
had made a nest for herself at the top of this
old house, where she had artistically
arranged all the pretty things which she
was not absolutely forbidden to touch, and
had introduced an amount of bright colouring
and strong effect which told its own word-
less tale, and you knew without asking that
the mistress of this tiny retreat had a
craving for the beautiful and the picturesque
which would surmount every other want in

life. A strong will ruled all her actions, a
will which her father, engrossed in the cares
of his business and the history of his art-
treasures, had never sought to stem. Her
mother had died when she was a mere baby,
and she had grown up in an atmosphere of
" sacred dust ; " pictures, and china, vertu
and bijouterie had been her playthings.
She had loved them as most children do their
dolls, talked to them, and told stories about
them founded on the facts her quick ears
had gathered from the many visitors and
lovers of art who dawdled away the mornings
among her father's treasures, and gossiped
with him over their beauties and their
histories. She had scarcely been educated
at all, yet she was not without knowledge ;
living under the patronage and shadow of
art, how could she fail to know something
and to yearn for more ? Her oriental descent
showed itself in the poetical, almost rhapsodi-
cal view from which she not unfrequently
regarded both people and things, overcoming
as it did the natural cunning peculiar to

her race, which would have taught her
to turn trifles to her own advantage.

So the old man and the girl sat down to
their evening meal, which, thanks to Mimi's
care, was well served, nor did the cooking
in any way disgrace the old foreign servant
who had the sole charge of the Jacobsens'
limited establishment.   Although Mimi had
professed to be very tired when she was
questioned by her father on the subject, she
seemed to have forgotten all about it, for
she talked and laughed so joyously, almost
excitedly, that the old man had scarcely a
chance of speaking.   He eat his supper
almost in silence, only occasionally smiling
when his daughter chattered on with a volu-
bility which was unlike her usually somewhat
taciturn nature.   To-day, for the first time,
she had seen a book full of "*fleurs animées*,"
and her vivid imagination was giving each of
her girl-friends her flower, then arranging
them and grouping them in her mind with
that love of redundancy and colouring
which came to her as a breath from her

eastern home. The old Jew listened with enjoyment to these vagaries of his daughter.

> "'Un pauvre bucheron tout couvert de ramée,
>   Sous le faix du fagot, aussi bien que des ans.'

You know the fable, Mimi; before you begin your gallery of beauty show how it must all end. Sketch then your old father amid the dry and withered sticks which shall be for him a frame work, it is what all these beautiful flowers and garlands must come to, my child."

For a moment a cloud passed over Mimi's face, but then she answered briskly,

" As the rods blossomed at Aaron's will, so will life and beauty return again to the aged stems, my father. I revere old age, and would, as you say, give it a prominent place in my gallery, but not as a warning or a regret."

" What then would you satirise ? What does your young knowledge tell you is the worst thing on earth, my child ? "

" Deceit," she answered, briskly.

" Draw it, Mimi ; it pleases me to hear you talk."

" A young and beautiful maiden, with dark hair and rich colouring, graceful in form, round in limb, velvety and soft and downy ; and for a flower-type I would take the Moorish cucumber, which from its slender threadlike stems hangs its luscious-looking blood-red head. It is so tempting that you long to cull the dainty morsel, yet it imbues with its poisonous attributes the very air you breathe."

Old Jacobsen looked astonished at his daughter's words, for there was earnestness and fervour in her voice, while a deep colour mantled her cheek, and her eyes shone brightly. When she had finished speaking she laid her head for a second on the table, and two or three convulsive sobs burst forth as though unbidden."

" What ails you, child, wherefore this emotion ? "

She looked up again, smiling amid the

tears she strove so courageously to repress—
the storm had been of short duration.

"I am only tired," she said. "I have
had a long day of pleasure. I shall be
better after a good sleep."

"Still devoted to pleasure, child," answered the old man, with a sneer, "for
me I shall be pleased when a new epoch
shall arrive; we have too much of these
Gentiles, Mimi."

For a moment she looked as though tears
were going to fall anew, but she restrained
them with an effort.

"Oh, father! how can you say so? why,
Christians are our best friends. How very
kind they have always been to me! They
seem quite to forget that I am only a poor
Jewish maiden living in this old garret, and
they take me out and *fête* me and pamper
me till my head is almost turned.

"Shrewdness is an instinct of your race,
—are you deficient in it, child?"

"No," she said, throwing up her head
proudly as though nettled at the insinuation,

"I can fend for myself in life, have no fear for me, father."

"I like it not, I like it not," muttered old Jacobsen to himself, as though unheeding her words. "Why crave the one ewe lamb from the poor man's fold? 'Behold the Lord shall raise up evil against them out of their own house' for this thing."

"My father, what madness is this,—is it a curse?" cried the girl, starting to her feet, while her whole frame dilated, "they are my friends, would give me the best they have on earth."

"We want not their gifts, Mimi. Israel's daughter has nothing to give in return to these Gentiles among whom we sojourn."

"You barter and cheapen and traffic with them," she said bluntly.

"Ja, ja, ja," he answered, rubbing his delicate hands together with nervous excitement, "this is my calling. Shall not the Gentile's gold flow into the coffers of the chosen people?"

"You are then very rich, my father?"

"I have it not said—I have it not said—all things on earth have their comparison; not rich like some of these English lords who come to buy my toys."

"English lords, yes, I envy them sometimes in their great palaces, surrounded as they are with plenty and luxury. I wish we could live in a better house than this, father."

The old man's bright eyes flashed.

"From your Christian friends you learn this foolishness, child. Rats burrow in dark holes and out-of-the-way corners, and they grow fat and strong; in the light of day, in the dwellings of man, they would be worried by ferrets and dogs."

"I never get worried or beset when I go into the world," said the girl, laughing, "I tell you they make so much of me, I am sometimes quite bewildered."

"Hein! hein! I like it not, I tell you," he continued. "My days of work are nearly numbered. I shall journey soon to the fold of Abraham—make that no Christian shall touch my hardly-gained earnings, or the curse of the God of Israel—"

"Hush, father, hush," she cried, "no more. Keep your riches, give them to the chief Rabbi for his poor, but bind me by no oath, heap no curse upon my head. I could not bear its weight, it would blight my young life, and I should droop and die."

"Foolish child I would not curse you, but the Gentile who would touch my gold."

"Enough, enough, let us speak of it no more," she said, going up to him and kissing him, "you will live long years yet to guard your riches, I hope, my father, and for the rest the God of Jacob will provide."

"'Tis well, child, 'tis well, but wherefore come these Gentiles? There has been here to-day a fair-spoken, sleek-faced woman who would fain have had speech of you, and with pertinacity refused to confide to me her business. She had none, she would have me believe, but to make your acquaintance only. Wherefore, Mimi? You are but a half-blossomed hedge-flower, this woman, seemingly of importance in her own eyes, can have no good design."

"Who was she, father? Did she leave no name?" and there was a visible agitation in Mimi's voice as she asked the question.

"Do the rag-pickers and bone-seekers give their names when they haunt your premises in search of booty?" he asked sneeringly.

"I do not know who the lady could be. I have invited no one," murmured the girl, "she must have been merely a client who came to see your bric-à-brac, father."

"Hein, hein! 'Alte Vögel fängt man nicht mit der Lockpfeife;'* she came for no good—no good I tell you, child. The Christian harpies are like vultures, ever flying about the dying man, and waiting with impatience for the little flicker of life to expire, that their revolting meal may begin. My gold! they think already that

* Old birds are not to be caught with chaff.

they hear it chink, for you are foolish, child, too foolish in your tenderness. You are no true daughter of Israel."

"Oh, father! these are hard words and cut me to the very soul; unsay them if you love me, father."

"Not so, Mimi, it is my love that bids me warn you of the evil hour that must arrive, when the Jewish maiden lends too willing an ear to Christian flatteries. Beware of them, child, spurn them, loathe them. Hedge yourself in with the prickly thorns of satire, and never be betrayed into trusting a Christian's oath."

"Father, father! it is too much—I cannot bear it; for this night at least spare me. Remember they are human, of the same flesh and blood as we are; why should they be so hardly judged?"

A low howl, like that of some wild animal, burst from the old man at these words.

"Is the girl bewitched?" he cried, "have the idolatrous demons taken possession of her? But no matter, the path is clear, the Mammon worshippers shall be balked of their prey. Gold is all they seek, and truly my curse shall follow the Gentile who shall touch my treasures."

With these words he left the room, and Mimi sank back in her chair almost fainting, and as though utterly powerless to cope with the old man's wrath.

CHAPTER XI.

WHEN THE FOOTLIGHTS ARE OUT.

PETTITA had been three or four days in Belgrave Street, and life with her was flowing on very evenly and pleasantly. She had not seen Richard Griesnach again since the evening he had dined at Mrs. Leigh's; he had spent the two or three following days "mewed up to his heaviness" in the privacy of the Temple; true, he had had several visits from Mr. Jenkins about the 'Educational Argus,' but as all the preliminaries for starting that erudite journal were not arranged, Mr. Griesnach's editorial powers had not yet been fully called into requisition, so he resolved to go off to Woodlands, and take counsel with Margaret.

Meanwhile, Pettita was amusing herself seeing life, and life under Bertha Leigh's guidance presented many and varied aspects. She had friends and acquaintances of every distinctive class, from the exalted aristocrats of Lady Bluntisfield's type (though, be it said, there were but few of these upon her list), down to the shadiest denizens of Bohemia. In fact, Bertha showed such a decided preference for these " back-stair acquaintances," as she termed them, that it was almost a pity she did not give up the struggle for " place," and save herself from the slanderous epithets which she felt society was perpetually ejaculating to her cost, and the knowledge of which, although she heard them not, kept her in a constant state of inward worry and torment.

True to her promise of having a professional opinion on the subject of Pettita's histrionic talent, the little brougham bore them one afternoon to a dingy house on the outskirts of the Regent's Park.

Bertha sent in a message to know if Mrs. Kelly would see her, and they were at once shown into an untidy-looking parlour; books, music, pictures, and photographs being littered all over it in a confusion which was not without its charm. Their owner evidently lived among them, they were her daily, nay, hourly companions, and she never could bear to have them put away out of her sight. She had a staring, stiffly-furnished, half-empty room in which she received state visits, but Bertha was a favourite, and had begged so hard to have the *entrée* of Mrs. Kelly's private "den," that she had succeeded in obtaining a privilege accorded but to few.

Pettita was delighted.

"Oh! if Margaret would only let me have a room like this, and not put everything away the moment one has done with it, how nice it would be?" she cried.

"Margaret has a regular mind," answered

Mrs. Leigh, laughing, "she could not live in the hopeless tangle in which you are perpetually involved."

"Is Mrs. Kelly in a tangle too?" asked Pettita, looking up wonderingly.

"Not now, she has lived long enough to unravel the skein. But here she is."

Pettita opened her large eyes and looked on in a sort of speechless awe. To this young country girl, whose only knowledge of "Her Majesty's servants" was from books, this real, living, breathing actress was a wonder. There was something, too, about Mrs. Kelly which was very taking, though she was no longer young. She was tall and slim and graceful, with a very pleasing face, while her dress, though by no means costly, was arranged with an artistic elegance which gave you an idea that posing for effect had become a second nature. Some white lace about her head was arranged *à la* Siddons, and enhanced the characteristic expression of her countenance.

She came into the room with a little bound, and was more demonstrative than perhaps was strictly in accordance with the dignity of her bearing, but this probably was owing to the exigencies of her profession.

Mrs. Leigh was received with effusion. She always managed by some witchery, of which she knew the secret, to gain an immense ascendancy over all those of her acquaintance who were just below her in the social scale. Pettita was of course introduced forthwith, but Mrs. Leigh did not at once enter on the real object of their visit. She had all Mrs. Kelly's private and public joys and sorrows to inquire about; Bertha, thorough tactician that she was, never forgot that the chief secret in the art of fascinating others is to identify yourself thoroughly with their hopes and fears. So they chatted on for a long time, Pettita listening without speaking, for Mrs. Kelly's clear articulation and the euphony of her tones as she related various little adventures which had befallen her, did not fail to make their mark.

At last Mrs. Kelly strayed away from the personal affairs, in which Mrs. Leigh seemed to take so deep an interest, and as she casually mentioned the name of "Sir Edward Bazalgette" Bertha suddenly recalled the business which had brought them there. She evidently was not desirous that Pettita should hear the revelations about Prince Charming which Mrs. Kelly might vouchsafe, so she started up.

"We really must go," she exclaimed, "in your agreeable society one forgets the flight of time. By the by, this child here is crazy to follow in your footsteps, and wreathe herself in dramatic laurels."

"Amateur theatricals—well, they are a charming amusement," said Mrs. Kelly, as she took Pettita's little gloved hand and held it warmly between both her own, "they have more self-satisfaction than belongs to the real stage, and none of the sting."

"You mistake," said Pettita, somewhat timidly, colouring up, "I cannot afford to play, I must work for my living."

"Then choose some other career," was the decided answer, gravely given.

Pettita looked very crestfallen, she had hoped at least for encouragement and approval from Mrs. Kelly.

"Then every one is against me,—what am I to do?" she said, in a choked voice, which showed that tears were fast rising.

"Better make skirts in an attic than venture on a career so fraught with difficulties, temptations, and annoyances, as is that of an actress. I have had a long eventful life, many laurels and many vexations, and had I a daughter of my own, I would shut her in a convent rather than she should go through all that I have done."

"Why, Mrs. Kelly and Margaret would quite agree," cried Pettita. "This is not at all what I had expected."

"I do not kown who Margaret may be, my child," continued Mrs. Kelly earnestly, "but whoever she is, if she is advising you to keep your freshness from the tarnishing glare of the footlights, she is acting towards you the part of a good and wise counsellor. I am not alluding to your talent or want of talent; I know nothing about it. You may be gifted with the genius of a Rachel; but it is from the life of false excitements, the desperate mental convulsions, torturing alike to both soul and body, I would save, if possible, any young thing who came to me for advice."

"And yet Mrs. Leigh tells me you are yourself a great actress," said Pettita naively.

Mrs. Kelly smiled.

"I have tasted fame and sigh for peace," she said gently. "If you persist in believing the stage to be your vocation, you will, should you live as long as I have, be as weary as I am now."

"What a dreary, dreary picture!" sighed

the girl, turning in a sort of piteous way to Mrs. Leigh.

She, however, only began to laugh. Bertha had evidently some little plan of her own about Pettita's future, and she did not exactly want this plunge into professional life to be carried out, at all events not yet. She meant it to be played with for a time, while other matters were ripening. If the girl failed to accomplish the end Bertha had in view, well, then it was very immaterial to her what became of her.

"I am afraid you are suffering from a slight attack of dyspepsia, my dear Mrs. Kelly," she said, as she looked at the actress, whose usually cheerful, lively manner had been so suddenly chilled into grave disapprobation by Pettita's appeal, "we must come some other day, child, when we hope Mrs. Kelly will not be so cold in the cause of her art, and may, perhaps, therefore kindly give us a few valuable hints."

"Pardon, dear lady," was the warm

answer, "you have totally misunderstood my meaning. I will gladly do anything in my small power to assist you and your young friend. If she be really bent on following my profession, every nerve shall be strained to place her to the best advantage, but I would have her ponder well over my words of warning. When once she has made the plunge, she must either swim or sink; it is useless to try and clamber back into the ship, for the ladder will have been carried away by the tide. However, do not look so downcast, little one," she continued, with that sudden change of voice training had so thoroughly mastered, "I am, perhaps, drawing what our dear friend, Mrs. Leigh, would call 'a dyspeptic picture.' Come to me to-morrow morning for an hour, alone, and we will see artistically, not socially, of how much further consideration the subject is worth, —that will assuredly weigh for something in the balance."

"Thank you, Mrs. Kelly, how good, how

very good you are!" and Pettita, gushing
with youthful enthusiasm, threw her arms
round the tall stately looking actress'
neck, and kissed her.

It was returned cordially. Freshness
and beauty and joy could not fail to
be appreciated by one whose nature was
so antagonistic to artifice or voidness as
was Mrs. Kelly's. Strange she had not
detected the false key-note in Bertha's
character. Who knows? perhaps she had,
but a woman of the world, as Mrs. Kelly
from her position was forced to be, does not
always find it politic to pass severe strictures
on her friends. Mrs. Kelly, too, was of a
sweet, amiable temperament, she would
rather have found an excuse for a flagrant
fault than have sought out a venial one
which its possessor strove to keep partially
hidden.

"Run away, child, and get into the
brougham," said Mrs. Leigh, when the
embrace was over, "if you are not de-

lighted with your morning's work you
ought to be."

Pettita did as she was bid, and Bertha
lingered behind for a few parting words
with Mrs. Kelly.

"You could not have done better if I
had prompted you," she whispered, "don't
encourage her too much at first, but see
what stuff she is made of. I doubt myself
if she will ever rise above burlesque."

Mrs. Kelly shook her head and looked
grave.

"Then do not let the dew be dashed off
her petals. She is a bonnie child and evidently comes of a good race."

"Ye-s, oh, yes!" said Mrs. Leigh, with
that quiet inflection of hers which always
raised a doubt. She thought of the Lima
mother,—but it were wiser not to admit the
fact, it might prove disadvantageous in
other matters. No one knew it but Richard
Griesnach, and he would never tell, so she
went on,

"She is of a very good family—decidedly—

her father was in the navy,—one of the St. Ormes,—but poor, poor as church mice. By the by, do not mention anything about Ted Bazalgette and his affairs before her,— he is a sort of connection, so mischief might come of it."

"I understand," said Mrs. Kelly, smiling.

She was a clever woman if she did understand either that or any other of Bertha's amalgamations, but it was as well, perhaps, that she asked no questions, for Bertha would have found it rather difficult to explain the connection which existed between the St. Ormes and the Bazalgettes. It answered her purpose, however, for the moment.

By this time she was standing by the street-door, which Mrs. Kelly held open herself. She gave one glance to see if Pettita were safe in the carriage out of earshot, then dropping her voice into a low whisper, she said hurriedly,

"I have traced the girl; she is a Jewess,

but I have not yet seen her,—she lives in such a dirty hole."

Mrs. Kelly bent her head and smiled again, this time without speaking. She knew a good deal of the rough hard side of life, and she was tolerably accustomed to breathing an atmosphere tainted with intrigue and chicanery, thus she was not so scrupulous or so fearful of soiling her fingers, or her reputation, as the case might be, as she would otherwise have been; yet there still remained a strong sense of principle, as it were instinct in Mrs. Kelly, and she never put herself out of the way to meddle detrimentally in other men's matters. "Let every struggler shift for himself as well as he can in this world," was her motto. She was therefore just a little bit surprised at this woman, who condescended to walk out of her frame, which though it hung rather low and not in the best light, yet had its place on the privileged walls of the Upper Ten. "A position so many poor aspirants are crazy for," thought Mrs. Kelly,

" and yet this lady every now and then
marches right away to track poor girls, who
have never interfered with her, into dirty
dens, and comes here for all sorts of information about people, which she thinks she
would never obtain if she sat quietly at
home by her own fireside.   There must be
some strong motive actuating her, though ;
she takes a lively interest in the affairs of
so many people.   It rather puzzles me,
sometimes."

These were the reflections that not unfrequently passed through Mrs. Kelly's brain
when Bertha Leigh and her little manœuvring ways came before her mind.   It never
entered the kind-hearted actress' head to
imagine, woman of the world though she
was, that Bertha craved to hold the secrets
of the lives of those around her, only that
she might make them dance as puppets at
her will ; yet Mrs. Kelly gave the information she so frequently came to seek from
her, grudgingly and scantily.   She did not
feel altogether sure of Mrs. Leigh's schemes,

though she was not sufficiently on her guard to seek either to frustrate or overthrow them. Bertha always seemed so kind and charming, that she could scarcely bring her mind to believe that her little combinations were anything but a harmless amusement. Too wary, however, to entangle herself more than was necessary, Mrs. Kelly only smiled, and asked no questions about the Jewish girl. She had too many occupations in life to waste her time, or in fact to be amused by a gossippy conversation relative to some girl she had never seen or was ever likely to see, although for some reason Bertha Leigh seemed to take an immense amount of interest in her,—for weal or woe had yet to be proved.

So Bertha got into the carriage, and that morning's work was accomplished, as far as Pettita was concerned, very satisfactorily; for, if she had not at once secured for herself that entrance to dramatic life which in her ignorance she had imagined was so easily attained, she had at least made the acquaintance of a loyal sterling woman, one who was held in high respect by all who knew her, and who was capable of proving a safer conductor through the mazes of life than Mrs. Leigh was ever likely to be, fine lady though she was.

CHAPTER XII.

HEN AND DUCKLING.

MRS. LEIGH and Pettita had returned to the little house in Belgrave Street and were sitting in a subdued light by the fire, sipping their five o'clock tea and chatting in the confidential though frequently treacherous way peculiar to women, over the events of the morning generally and the visit to Mrs. Kelly in particular.

They had come home from their drive rather earlier than usual, because Pettita's first visit to the theatre was to take place that very evening under the safe conduct of Sir Edward Bazalgette, whose services

Bertha had especially retained for the occasion.

"Dear! there is the visitor's bell,—how tiresome! we shall never be dressed in time," cried Pettita, starting up from the negligent attitude in which she had been lolling.

Mrs. Leigh smiled. Was it the expected play or the society of the cavalier that Pettita was looking forward to with so much impatience, she wondered. She had not time, however, to pursue the train of her thoughts for the door was thrown open, and to the intense surprise of both the ladies, Margaret walked into the room in her rapid decided way.

"Miss St. Orme, I am delighted to see you, but this visit is somewhat unexpected," said Mrs. Leigh more stiffly than was her wont when receiving guests in her own house. If the truth were told she nearly lost her temper when she saw Margaret, whose presence she regarded very much in the light of an intrusion.

Pettita, however, rushed into her sister's

arms, and kissed her in her warm impulsive way.

"What has brought you, Madge dear, the cottage is not burnt down by chance, is it ?"

"I want you to come back with me, Pettita, I am very lonely without my child, so I came off suddenly to fetch you; there is plenty of time to catch the seven o'clock train."

"Margaret, you must be mad," cried Pettita, "I am certainly not going back with you to-night; it is quite impossible, I have no end of engagements."

"They surely will not stand in the way of your love for and obedience to your sister, Pettita."

"Obedience is a nasty word," retorted Pettita, whose little naughty temper was oozing out at the idea of being ordered home just when she was going to enjoy herself, "there is not a creature in the world to whom I am bound to be obedient; nowhere in the Bible are sisters mentioned, and as for love, if you love me as much as you profess to do, you would know when I am well off, and leave me in peace with Mrs. Leigh."

Margaret turned as pale as death.

Had she imagined the young sister was always to be subservient to her will? If so, how thoroughly had she been mistaken. The sudden awakening for a moment paralysed her, so much so that she could not trust herself to speak. Bertha, however, came to the rescue with those dulcet tones of hers.

"You will not think of returning home to-night, my dear Miss St. Orme; we are going to the play, and the child would be too disappointed if she were carried off. I have a tiny room which is entirely at your disposal, and we shall both be so glad if you will remain with us for a few days."

"Thank you," answered Margaret stiffly, drawing herself up with cold dignity, "but I have no wish to intrude my presence where I see I am not wanted. I cannot stop here, but I must say it is my wish for many reasons that my sister should return with me."

"Then she will not—do you understand that?—at least, not to-night," cried Pettita. "What a fool you are, Madge! you are always trying to make one uncomfortable and wretched; you don't know what it is to be jolly and happy. If duty and misery are the synonyms you always make them, keep them both all to yourself,—now sit down on that cosy sofa and listen to reason. As you have chosen to take this wild-goose chase after me, you must accept Mrs. Leigh's invitation for to-night. At least, *I* don't intend to give up my play,—besides, to-morrow—"

A frown and a pinch from Mrs. Leigh ended the sentence somewhat abruptly.

"To-morrow you will return with me if I concede the point and stay to-night?" asked Margaret gravely.

"Oh! do let to-morrow take care of it-

self," interrupted Bertha; " let us make ourselves as happy to-night as circumstances
will permit. I fear, however, you will find
it very dull here while we are out. My
dear Miss St. Orme, if you have any friend
you would like to invite to chat with you,
pray use my house as though it were your
own."

Margaret bowed.

" I have no friends in London," she said
coldly, "and I am never dull."

" You said just now you were dull at
Woodlands without me, though I did not
believe it," interrupted Pettita; " tell me
the truth, why have you come to town after
me ?"

"To prevent you, if possible, from degrading your father's name by dashing head-
long into a false career, and from storing up
unhappiness for your future life."

" Have you so little faith in me that you
could not trust me?" asked Bertha's little
soft voice, and she laid her hand as she
spoke on Pettita with a gentle squeeze,

which tacitly bade her be silent, and not break out either in harsh invectives or into a gushing flow of information.

" I scarcely know whom to trust," replied Margaret somewhat despondingly, " but I know my duty is to look after my sister, and I mean to fulfil it to the letter."

Pettita flushed up scarlet, and would not have been restrained much longer from pouring forth her wrath. It always did make her so very angry to be thought incapable of taking care of herself. Mrs. Leigh, however, suggested that she should run away upstairs and dress, while she had a little conversation with Margaret. As usual, Bertha succeeded in levelling the rough bits and pacifying Margaret's mind, for a time at least, on the subject of her sister's future career. When Mrs. Leigh, some quarter of an hour later, followed Pettita upstairs, she had fully persuaded Margaret to trust to her management about the stage, and quietly to place full reliance on her judgment and knowledge of the world. Just for one second she popped into Pettita's room.

"Not one word to your sister about Mrs. Kelly if you value my friendship, or her opinion," she said hurriedly.

"Oh! Mrs. Leigh, I don't like having secrets from Madge; after all, it was very good of her to come and look after me, and I don't think I treated her quite fairly or kindly."

Bertha shrugged her well-formed shoulders.

"As you like, but people who reveal everything generally lose their game. I should have imagined you could without difficulty have held your tongue till after your interview with Mrs. Kelly to-morrow, but perhaps Margaret is right, you are only a baby and not capable of acting for yourself."

The flash Mrs. Leigh knew these words were sure to raise came at once into the girl's eyes.

"You need not twit me so sharply," she

said, " I will prove I can be silent as death ;
poor Madge, I wish she had stayed at
Woodlands."

"So do I with all my heart," muttered
Bertha to herself as, having kissed Pettita,
she left her; and yet a combination under
her own roof, was it not the very thing
Bertha Leigh would have craved for ? only
she was not very sure of Pettita,—Sir
Edward Bazalgette, too, was coming to dinner.   Between the two Bertha was sorely
afraid that Margaret would see and hear far
more than was intended ; altogether it was
an amalgamation she would never have
brought about could she have helped it.

The dinner, however, went off more
cheerily than could have been expected, for
Margaret's still grave manner had always
more or less of a depressing effect, and had
not Bertha roused herself and talked gaily
and unweariedly to Sir Edward, almost to
the exclusion of both the sisters, it would
have been a dreary repast enough, and the
little spots marked " dangerous," which she

so perpetually and cleverly piloted them all away from, would inevitably have engulfed them long before the announcement came that the brougham was at the door.

At last they were off, and Margaret was left to pass the evening with a book and her thoughts for her only companions. True, Sir Edward had suggested that there was no reason as far as he—short-sighted individual —knew, why she should not go too, but Mrs. Leigh thought differently, and said there was, she regretted to say, no place, while one of her little frowns, which he understood so well, reminded him that the limited proportions of the box which he had himself taken could not by any means be stretched so as to hold another inmate.

For once Bertha Leigh had chosen wisely, and the play she had selected was a good drama of the legitimate school, the acting had the reputation of being above average merit, and the piece had been put on the stage carefully and with much scenic effect. Bertha herself would in all probability have

infinitely preferred witnessing a burlesque,
but she wanted to let Pettita see the best,
according to the critics, that London could
produce.

"We will not vitiate her taste at first
starting," she had said to herself as she ran
her eye down the theatrical advertisements
and selected this one.

Pettita was in a state of enthusiastic
excitement which to her companions was
unparalleled, accustomed as they were to
the *blasées* damsels who had lived among
glare and tinsel from their cradles, and who,
since they witnessed their first pantomime
at the age of six, had probably kept the ball
rolling pretty briskly, and therefore were
not likely to be so readily impressed as
was this country maiden. In vain did Sir
Edward seek to pour into Pettita's ear the
little honied phrases which were wont to
trip so glibly off his sugared tongue, she
scarcely either heard or saw him. He had
sunk into a very secondary position before
those heroes of the footlights. Bertha was

intensely amused, partly at Sir Edward's discomfiture, partly at Pettita's utter ingenuousness and the total absence of all conventional *ennui* which there was about the girl.

"Leave her, Ted," she said laughing, "she will talk to you when her astonishment over all this glitter has subsided. I would not be jealous of paper crowns if I were you."

"I have no right to be jealous at all," he answered somewhat sharply. "I wish you would not always speak as if you took it for granted that a feeling exists between me and this young friend of yours."

Bertha shook all over with that rippling laugh of hers.

"You are a good joke, my dear boy, indeed you are. What is the use of trying to deceive me. You know that you are over head and ears in love with Pettita St. Orme."

"And you know, Mrs. Leigh, that even were it so the whole thing is useless, and with that knowledge you ought to keep her as much as possible out of my way,—only, self-conceited though I usually am, I don't believe she cares a brass button about me," and he turned and looked at Pettita, who, entirely absorbed by what was going on on the stage had apparently quite forgotten that Sir Edward Bazalgette even existed.

What man who prides himself on his universal success with women, would not be piqued at finding that he is treated with indifference by a young half-fledged country girl? Nothing could have made him more eager in pursuit, especially too as he was spurred on by Bertha's laughs and little 'paper bullets.'

"Please don't talk to me, I want to watch the play," was the only answer he had received whenever he had addressed any observations to Pettita, so he had resolved to devote himself to Mrs. Leigh for the remainder of the evening, and to take his revenge on her friend at the very first opportunity that offered itself.

On a sudden however Bertha exclaimed,

"Good gracious! Ted, look, who is that sitting in the stalls? Lord Avebury, if I ever saw him in the flesh," and all the colour forsook her face as she raised her opera-glass to her eyes, partly to conceal her confusion, partly to assure herself that the owner of the stall was indeed the man she had taken him to be.

"Impossible! I had no idea he was in England," and Sir Edward followed at once in the wake of Bertha's excitement, and looked eagerly towards the stalls. "By Jove! it is, though, why, what the very deuce has brought him back again so soon?"

Was there? Yes, there was just an almost imperceptible shade of satisfaction on Bertha's face as she dropped her glass, and with recovered composure looked up somewhat mischievously at Sir Edward, whose evident annoyance seemed to amuse her.

"And to be at the play too, without making his arrival known to any one! I wonder when he came home. He has not called on you, has he, Mrs. Leigh?"

"On me?" she said, smiling sweetly, "why should he call on me the moment he arrives? I am not of his kith and kin."

"No, no, but you are very good friends, every one knows that."

"Lord Avebury's circle of acquaintance is a large one, he is a popular man," and she drew her opera-cloak round her, as though desirous of wrapping herself up in a general statement.

"As soon as the curtain falls I will go and speak to him. I am all curiosity to know why he has cut his winter abroad so very short. Shall I bring him up here?"

"If he wishes to come, I shall be very happy to see him."

And so at the end of the second act the ladies were left alone, and Bertha seemed almost as much absorbed in watching Sir Edward's appearance in the stalls, the hand-shaking between the two men, their short conversation, the rapid glance directed to her box, as had been Pettita by the play itself. Here was evidently another drama, being enacted under the girl's very eyes, though in her ignorance she knew it not.

Two minutes more and the gentlemen entered the box. Bertha sat back in her chair—calm and imperturbable-looking— a self-possessed woman of the world, who never allowed herself to show a sign, whatever might be the inward struggle.

The man they called Lord Avebury was no longer young, that is he had passed the meridian of life, but he was handsome. He had a frank open countenance, with just enough sternness about it to denote a strong will—and he was very martial-looking in his gait and bearing. There was a decided resemblance between him and the younger

man that stood beside him, their features
were of the same type—not surprising, for
Sir Edward was his sister's child, but for all
this the distance between them was im-
measurable. Neither in feature, form, nor
character did Sir Edward Bazalgette ap-
proach his uncle, who, as Mrs. Leigh had
truly said, was a popular man—one of those
mortals who understand the art of keeping
society perpetually at a distance—never
admitting anything like a familiarity—
and so retaining his power and place as
master.

"Has Lord Avebury turned a political
spy, or what has happened to him, that he
creeps back to England without letting any
of his friends know?" asked Bertha, smiling
as they shook hands.

"I returned only this very day. You
do not think I should have let twenty-four
hours pass without paying Belgrave Street
a visit?" he said gallantly. "As for this
young scapegrace here, I sent a note to tell
him of my arrival, but heard he had gone

out. I scarcely hoped to find him in such good company."

For a moment his eyes fell on Pettita, then he dropped into the empty chair by Mrs. Leigh.

"That girl, she is—"

"Ah! how remiss of me; allow me to introduce Miss St. Orme, a very dear young friend of mine—Lord Avebury."

Then there was a good deal of whispered conversation between Bertha and the new-comer, and as their glances were not unfrequently directed to Pettita and Sir Edward, it was obvious that they were the subject of their remarks.

The curtain had by this time been raised again, and to everything but what was passing on that marvellous stage Pettita was lost, but Ted Bazalgette, as his familiars called him, was obviously uncomfortable. If you could have peeped into his box of secret thoughts, you would assuredly have discovered that the one which lay uppermost was a strong wish that his uncle would

return to Italy and remain there for an in-
definite period. It was not that he disliked
him, far from it, it was the very love and
respect he had for him which made him
wince whenever he patted him familiarly on
the back, and avert his face whenever Lord
Avebury's frank honest eyes sought to read
him in a very disagreeable way they had,—
a way that was particularly perplexing
at times, and which Bertha, strong as
was evidently her regard for him, had
not failed frequently to find as difficult to
circumvent as did at this moment his
nephew.

At last, to Pettita's no small regret, the
play was over, and the general rush out
began. There is always a sort of "sauve
qui peut" idea about the way people hurry
from a place of public amusement the
moment the performance has been brought
to an end.

"You will come and eat a tiny sandwich
at my house, Lord Avebury—Sir Edward
has promised to accompany us," said Bertha's

soft voice, as the two cavaliers escorted her and Pettita to the brougham.

He bowed acquiescence, and half an hour later the quartette was enjoying the good things of life in the little dining-room in Belgrave Street. Nor was the party of the quietest, Mrs. Leigh with her peculiar facility for drawing people out and setting them entirely at their ease, seemed to have accomplished her work more effectually than usual this evening—and they talked and laughed over Lord Avebury's droll description of some foreign experiences, till the little house echoed again with their merriment. The shadows were all gone, even from Sir Edward's brow—the witching hour of night, the bright snug room, the beauty, the flowers, above all the wine— yes it was evidently one of Bertha's happiest combinations. She basked in a genial hour like the present, with no external influences to jar, and she sat there looking so plump and soft and white, that he must indeed have been a horrid disbeliever who could have ascribed to her anything but the sweetest, kindest, most womanly attributes.

There is a flavour of Bohemianism about these little supper parties, which makes them especially acceptable to the woman of society who likes to play with dangerous weapons, as a child would with fire, and who would shiver and look horrified if you called her "fast," but who is nevertheless just toppling on the verge of the abyss. Luck or circumstances, rather than principle, being about the only thing which will keep her from tumbling over.

To Pettita it was something quite new, and under the influence of her companion's vivacity she had assumed a half shy, half saucy, manner which from the entire absence of everything artificial about it was especially taking.

Altogether the evening had been a success, and, charmed with themselves and with each other, the *convives* separated far on

in the small hours, while Margaret was
asleep, dreaming of the young sister in
whom all her love was centred, and for
whom she would have given up everything
in life.

CHAPTER XIII.

EGYPT SPOILS ISRAEL.

THE people who visited old Jacobsen's *sanctum* of beauties were of very varied classes and dispositions. A rare mixture of the odds and ends of life was not unfrequently assembled there—such as one but rarely meets under the same roof and in the same room. Many patrons of art, who by former purchases had bought the right of *entrée*, pottered away their mornings while they pleased their senses, by looking at the pretty things which came in daily, collected as they were by some of Jacobsen's repulsive-looking satellites, who, in almost every quarter of the globe, cheapened the treasures which were eventually to find their way into the old man's net.

Against these Israelitish traffickers did the aristocratic element expect to jostle, but these lordlings were perhaps scarcely prepared for the queer little episodes which not unfrequently occurred, when unfortunate beings would bring in the gems and precious stones which want reduced them to part with, and which they hoped to turn into ready money at old Jacobsen's hands. Accidents of recognition would befall, meetings would sometimes take place which would make the old man, with his keen love of satirising the follies and foibles of his fellows, chuckle to himself as he rubbed his little womanish hands together.

To-day the Jew's den is especially crowded, —a work of art has arrived which is making a sensation among the critics. It is a large ebony cabinet in carving of exquisite design and workmanship; when thrown open the doors and interior of the case form seven panels, on which are painted in miniature the seven dolors of Our Lady.

This marvel of beauty is supposed to date from about the fifteenth century, when it had probably graced the private chapel of some rich Italian devotee. Now, after the lapse of years, during which it had been lost sight of, it had found its way into old Jacobsen's "treasure den," and was receiving veneration once again, though of a very different nature. Every one in that room did homage to the genius, which had created and worked out that marvellous art-design, there was no thought for the deeper meaning, no tribute offered to her who had suffered such cruel sorrows lest man's redemption should be lost. Altogether it was a strange sight in a Jew's abode—and if those gazing there had been less engaged with their criticisms, some of them at least must have testified to it.

The old man himself was in a state of exuberant spirits. He loved to see his house crowded with visitors, it was as a flattering unction to him that this throng of English aristocrats should be making their glib off-hand remarks in his *sanctum*, and treating him as the potentate who bought and dispersed at his will these beautiful subjects in art and gem. Bitterly as he reprobated the "Gentiles" whenever he was alone with Mimi, nothing could be more obsequious or more cringing than was his manner to them, when they paid him a visit; no wonder then that the girl thought they must be of a better race than he, for some reason, would have her suspect, and she had consequently made more than one Christian friend.

Usually when visitors are there Mimi is to be seen wandering about from one to the other, talking occasionally in her quiet grave way, but more frequently listening to the remarks going on around her, and drawing her own inferences from them. Thus the amount of general information she had picked up was very extensive, but unfortunately, side by side with it, there was a large share of gossip, which rendered her better acquainted with the movements and little scandals of the Upper Ten than was many a girl who lived in their very midst.

Several inquiries, however, had on this occasion been made after Mimi, who had not yet appeared. At last she might be seen coming slowly down the creaking old staircase. She entered the room, and without saluting any one, beyond a grave bend of her stately head in return for some recognition, she took her place among those standing round the cabinet. Several gentlemen who knew her well, addressed her, but she treated them as though she heard them not, and stood in a wrapt way looking at the beauties those open doors revealed. Eight-and-forty hours had not yet passed since she had listened to her father's curses and invectives on her Gentile friends, and, not able to shake off their weight, she had remained till now immured in the privacy of her own room, bowed down, as it were,

under an oppression from which she vainly
sought to free herself.   She had not, therefore, previously seen this work of art, which
had been unpacked but yesterday, and she
seemed quite entranced by it.   Her practised
eye, accustomed from childhood to look for
beauty, recognised at once the hand of a
master, but beyond this, in her present
perturbed state, the subject seemed to touch
her heart, and had it not been for the crowd
around she would probably have thrown
herself down in an agony of tears before the
suffering Virgin.

The power of self-control, however, was
one of her strongest points, and save for her
silence, no one would have imagined that
she was other than a cold, inflexible woman,
who from long usage was, with the critical
eye of a connoisseur, depreciating the beauties
she gazed on.

The hubbub of voices went on around,
men passed in the light careless way that is
their nature, from the sublime even to the
ridiculous—nay, lower still, to the profane,

for at last scandal raised its venomed tongue and many a racy little episode and pointed story was passed about in half whispers.

"Since when have you become a patroness of art? Is the house in Belgrave Street to be adorned with gems amongst other novelties?" said a man's voice, as Bertha Leigh, evidently to the surprise of those among the crowd who knew her, came smiling into the room, looking as bland and happy and soft as though such a thing as care were unknown on earth.

"Why should I be banished? Mr. Jacobsen's collection is so *berühmt*," she said, using one of the very few German words she knew, as she sidled up to the old Jew and held out her hand to him. "You will bid me welcome, will you not?"

He touched the tips of her fingers somewhat coldly, for he recognised in Bertha the same lady who had previously asked for Mimi; besides, he was scarcely in the habit of being shaken hands with by his customers.

"In trade, large buyers have the first place," he said quietly.

"What a sordid speech! but I know you do not mean it," cried Bertha, laughing.

He looked at her for a moment with his keen little eyes.

"What does miladi desire to see?" he asked. Old Jacobsen called all his English customers milord or miladi.

"Everything pretty that you have to show," she answered, "including your daughter, of whom I have heard much from a friend of mine, and whose acquaintance, as I told you two or three days ago, I would so gladly make."

"The child were better in her garret singing praises and tuning her harp, like the Jewish maidens of old time, than learning the workings of a world in which she can never dwell. Against my will she seeks for pleasure in strange haunts."

"I am very sorry you disapprove of her going out; I will not try to beguile her, but may I not at least speak to her?"

"As you will, miladi; I am but a poor Jew at your service," and he bowed profoundly. Then in a loud tone he called to Mimi, who was still standing lost in contemplation of the cabinet. She started as she heard her father's voice, and turning round confronted Mrs. Leigh.

That she was not entirely a stranger to Mimi was very obvious, from the look that instantly came into her eyes when she saw her, but she made no farther sign, only bowed when Bertha in her blandest tones, and with her kindest, most patronising manner, told her how glad she was to make her acquaintance. She had heard so much of her beauty and her enthusiasm for art, from their mutual friend Miss Fenton.

"My father forbids me to associate in future with those who are not of my race and station. I shall go to Miss Fenton's no more," said Mimi coldly.

"And do you always obey your father in everything? What a model daughter! You must at least make an exception in my favour, and initiate me in the formulæ of a race whose children arrive at such perfect obedience."

Mimi winced and coloured up under this somewhat pointed speech.

"The Jews are, perhaps, not better than the Christians," she said in a very low tone. "If we could only be left to do our work as we see it is for the best, it would be a happiness."

"Nay, child, you ask what is impossible on earth. Interference is one of the motive powers of the world. Infringement on what we consider our personal rights is what we all have to make our little fight against, as best we can."

"It is the want of understanding other people's reasons and feelings which makes life so difficult," answered Mimi wearily. "I often wish I were dead, if one only knew what would come after."

"Have you no room of your own where we can talk?" asked Bertha, as she took the young Jewess by the hand; "I would

so gladly be of use to you, and if I mistake
not I can be so."

Mimi led the way upstairs, and Mrs.
Leigh followed smiling. Here was a more
pliable impressionable nature than from
the grand-looking young Jewess' imposing
beauty she had at first been led to expect.

And so in the privacy of Mimi's pretty
room they sat together and talked their
woman's talk. Bertha, assuming her most
interested manner, drew the girl out till she
made her tell her of her father's wrath,
and his bitter invectives on her Christian
friends.

"I will not go to Miss Fenton's house
again at present," she said; "perhaps that
will appease him somewhat."

"Ah! I see," suggested Mrs. Leigh;
"Marcia Fenton has more power over you
than your father judges expedient."

"No, I do not think that it is against her
that his anger is directed, but against Mr.
Fenton. My father and he have frequent
business relations. They both trade in

money, though Mr. Fenton deals much more largely in that way than my father, and I have reason to believe that there has been lately a dispute between them. For the moment he would include all Christians in his anger, and I must humour his whims and abide the time when they shall have passed."

Mrs. Leigh elevated her well-shaped eyebrows, and smiled meaningly at these words.

"Of course, you have no suspicion of the cause of the quarrel between Mr. Fenton and your father?"

"I have told you it is money. What care I to enter into their business secrets? It is not my province." But Mimi's voice trembled slightly as she answered, and her face paled visibly, while her fingers were clutched nervously together in her lap. Bertha laid her warm soft hand upon them.

"My child, you are right," she said, in a low confidential tone. "I have come to warn you; keep to the privacy of your own home—avoid for the present your Christian friends; if your father should suspect the interest you have in the matter, it will bring trouble and difficulties to one you love."

"To one I love?" exclaimed Mimi, starting up; "how do you know I love any one, whom do you mean? I have seen you once, it is true, but I do not even know your name! How can you venture, then, to come and talk to me of my private affairs?"

"You saw me once, yes, when I was walking with Sir Edward Bazalgette, whom I have known from childhood, and the members of whose family are among my oldest friends—now do you understand why I have come to seek you out?"

Mimi bent her head down low upon her breast, to avoid meeting Bertha's searching gaze.

"No!" she said, "for I don't believe Sir Edward sent you. He never mentioned you to me, and he always advised me to mistrust all female friends."

"Then, there is an understanding between you," said Bertha quietly.

That little unguarded word *then* aroused the Jewess' suspicions, and prevented Mrs. Leigh for the moment at all events from hearing more.

Mimi raised her head and looked up proudly.

"What information you require you must seek from Sir Edward himself. I have none to give."

"Silly, silly child!" said Bertha, trying to recover the ground she had let slip from under her. "I suspect I know far more of Sir Edward and his affairs than you do yourself. How frequently has he talked over with me both the money difficulties in which he is involved with your father, and his admiration for you!"

"Did he send you here?" asked Mimi suddenly.

"Well, not exactly; but can you not understand the longing that one may have to be better acquainted with an individual of whom one's best friends talk so warmly and so frequently?"

"It were wiser to be silent," said the girl, with a cold scorn in her voice, which showed Bertha that to mould Mimi Jacobsen to her will, and make her believe in her, would be no easy task; however, she went on with her pretty platitudes.

"Were it not for this money-storm, which seems so thick in the atmosphere of your home just now, I would invite you to my house, where we could all meet and pass some pleasant hours together, but under the circumstances I fear we must postpone the happiness. Take my advice, dear child, keep very quiet for the present; seek to see none of your friends, for a week or two at least. In the meantime, if you can have sufficient faith in almost a stranger, rely on me for information."

"Thank you, lady, thank you for your kindness. I shall probably hear from my father how these business matters proceed.

He has but few secrets from me," and her head sank once more into her lap.

"Your father is the last person likely to be made acquainted with the necessity Sir Edward may find to leave the country," suggested Bertha quietly.

"Leave the country—he—Edward Bazalgette?—impossible!—and on account of persecution from my father,—and I am powerless to help. Oh, this is too much!" and her whole frame shook under the violence of her emotion.

"Do not give way thus, my child; the game is not lost yet, though a false move on your part now may prove fatal. You must do nothing, absolutely nothing. If your father were to suspect your interest in the matter, he would be doubly desirous of crushing Sir Edward."

But Mimi did not answer, only sat sobbing on us though there were no comfort left in life. Vainly did Bertha strive to soothe her; the young heart, which was only for the first time beginning to feel the burden and heat of the fierce sun of life, refused to be consoled; perhaps, too, Mimi had her own secret reasons for being more crushed and desponding than the outward appearance of passing events seemed to warrant. At last, however, the extreme violence of her grief spent itself, and she answered Mrs. Leigh's caressive little speeches more genially than she had hitherto done. It is, after all, more or less of a comfort to have a kind shoulder on which to lay your aching head; and a soft voice bidding you have faith and trust is not without its influence. So Mimi yielded, and consented to leave her future in Bertha Leigh's hands, who promised to work it out for her to the best of her power, and in the manner most conducive to her happiness and *his*.

"You will see him, then, dear lady, and tell him why I have broken my tryst, and cannot come to the old place of meeting; and you will beg him, for my sake, to make the best terms he can with my father."

Bertha kissed her lovingly, and promised that she would talk to Sir Edward, and in two or three days come and see Mimi again, and give her information as to how matters were progressing.

Thus they parted,—and with insidious falseness Bertha had begun the first act in a little drama which, for some private reasons of her own, she had determined if possible to play out.

And Mimi sat there long and passively, as though ossified by the cold weight of thought. A few months ago she had been a light, joyous girl, the sunshine of her father's heart, the light of his old home; but events had changed the current of her life, age and care and depression seemed to have come upon her even in the heyday of her youth, and though with a vigorous effort she would cast them from her when in her father's presence, and would laugh and chatter excitedly for his amusement, it was simply as one acting a part, and anxious if possible to lull any suspicions which might

have been aroused. For two long hours
after Mrs. Leigh's departure she sat there,
till the complete stillness which had crept
over the house seemed to awaken in her the
knowledge that action of some sort was a
necessity, if she would not be questioned.
She had only just risen from her crouching
position, and was beginning to bestir herself
about some woman's work, when the door
opened and her father entered.

CHAPTER XIV.

TO THE ABBEY!

AFTER Bertha Leigh had quitted Mimi Jacobsen on the morning following the supper-party in Belgrave Street, she drove round in the little brougham to the Regent's Park to call for Pettita, who had meanwhile been having a private interview with Mrs. Kelly. There was a flush on the girl's face, a pink look about her pretty eyes, as she took her seat in the carriage.

"Another excited heroine," thought the more self-composed Bertha, "all these strong emotions must have a very bad effect on the constitution. Well, child," she said out loud, "have you been put through your paces and found wanting, that you look so woebegone ? Never mind, I really do think rushing on the stage to make money is only the sort of thing one reads of in a book, it is scarcely practicable in real life—but you *would* have a peep into the possibilities of following such a career."

Pettita began to cry.

" I should not care if I could get money to help Madge. Do you think, Mrs. Leigh, that I would have deceived her by coming out without telling her where I was going, if I had not hoped to help her ? When I saw her grave pale face at breakfast this morning, I longed to rush into her arms and tell her everything. How sorry I was I had spoken sharply last night, and had not given up the play at once, and gone home with her if she wished it, for she is a dear good, kind old Madge, and loves me very much, though it is very hard sometimes for me, wicked by nature as I am, to understand how she can sacrifice everything to duty in the way she does."

"Good gracious! Pettita, do stop and allow me a little breathing space in the midst of these rhapsodies over your sister's goodness, which I am sure no one denies, though what in the world it has to do with Mrs. Kelly and your wish to go on the stage I cannot comprehend."

"Everything, for Madge is to go and see Mrs. Kelly, and they are to talk about me, though Mrs. Kelly, who is almost as good and nice as Madge, says she is sure they will neither of them consent to my being an actress."

"They both make a great fuss about nothing," said Bertha, with a little frown. "I cannot see why you should not go on the stage as well as—"

"Do you wish it for me?" asked Pettita, not heeding the unended sentence.

"No, I wish you for the next few weeks to remain quietly with me. You are happy with me, are you not, Pettita?"

"Very," cried the girl, throwing her arms round Bertha's neck and kissing her.

" Well, then, we must persuade Margaret after a visit of a few days, to go back to Woodlands and finish her packing. In the meantime you will stop with me, as previously arranged, and we will not even discuss the dreary subject of what you are eventually to do. Chance, little one, or, as I suppose Margaret would call it, Providence plays a very conspicuous part in all our lives, so suppose you wait a bit and see if a trump card will turn up. You are young and beautiful, but remember, perpetually tormenting yourself about the future will soon make an ugly old frump of you, so let us be jolly while we may."

Even the bright vista which life for the next two or three months at Mrs. Leigh's presented, was scarcely sufficient to comfort Pettita, whose better feelings had been aroused, and the warm impulsiveness of her nature excited to its utmost by Mrs. Kelly's straightforward truth, as she placed the future before Pettita with all the shrewdness of a practical woman of the world,

and all the loyalty of a high-principled
one.

"Oh! but I have my work to do—fun
and amusement is not the only end in life.
Why should Madge slave all alone? it is
my duty to help her!"

"Pettita, don't be tiresome and provoking!" cried Mrs. Leigh, losing her
placidity,—scarcely her temper, that was
always kept in great subjection. "Margaret's only care and anxiety is on your
account. You will annoy her far more by
making a public exhibition of yourself than
by remaining immured in the privacy of
noodledom all your life. When she hears
you have given up the stage, she will be
quite happy and contented, and if you cannot make yourself the same in my house for
the next few weeks, well, you are an ungrateful little ape, that is all I have to
say."

Thus far it was settled between them, but
Bertha was destined to be still farther provoked, for on reaching Belgrave Street in

time for a late lunch, they found Richard
Griesnach in the drawing-room in close
conversation with Margaret. Mrs. Leigh's
first impulse was to rush to her room and
shut herself up till all this tiresome talk,
which she had brought upon herself by
taking possession of the girl should have
come to an end; but for some reason of her
own she intended to stand her ground, so,
having shaken hands with the little man,
she sank down wearily in the corner of the
sofa, while Pettita, in her effusive way,
gave an account of her morning's experiences.

Bertha, annoyed as she was at what she
called "the platitudes of these self-righteous
people," could not help being amused by
Margaret's intense look of surprise and
horror at all she heard; and at her prompt
and decided refusal to become acquainted
with Mrs. Kelly Bertha fairly laughed.

"Oh! young woman who knows nothing
of life," she said, "you see I have done the
best for your sister, for under my guidance

she has given up the stage of her own will,
while you would probably have drilled her
and lectured her till you had driven her on
to it. Now for goodness' sake do not let us
hear anything more about it, but as a com-
pensation for all this uninteresting talk you
are going to leave me Pettita as first agreed,
and we are going to play a little comedietta
of real life."

Margaret still had her misgivings about
the air of Belgrave Street being good for
Pettita, but how could she with her cramped
means find it in her heart to take her away,
now that there seemed no actual present
danger to terrify her, and that Richard
Griesnach urged that she should remain,
and promised to watch over her ?

A promise at which Mrs. Leigh's eyebrows arched slightly. She had no intention
of sharing with any one, least of all with
Mr. Griesnach, the duties of chaperone.
So with a few more words Margaret rose to
depart, she had decided to leave her sister,
thus there was no more to be said; before

Bertha Leigh she was not likely to bestow on Pettita one of her grave kind lectures, for Margaret always felt rather uncomfortable in Bertha's presence, and was impressed with a sort of inward conviction that she was being laughed at. Certainly these two women were antipathetic.

Pettita almost broke down when she saw her good old Madge really start off on her journey back to Woodlands, having refused all Mrs. Leigh's reiterated invitations that she should remain for a few days. And when the door fairly closed on them both, for Richard Griesnach insisted on accompanying Margaret to the station, and Bertha burst out into one of those ringing laughs with which she only occasionally indulged herself, Pettita stamped her foot, and in her impetuous off-hand way declared her to be both " unkind and unfeeling."

But Mrs Leigh only went on laughing.

" A marriage, Pettita, a marriage between those two ! Would it not be charming ?"

"What nonsense," cried Pettita indignantly; "you are always making up something. I am sure Madge will never marry; besides, fancy any one marrying 'old Dick.' He is a dear kind creature, but to think of marrying him,—that is too preposterous."

"Well, I must own he would suit Margaret the better of the two. Yet I have sometimes had a fancy that he was falling in love with you."

Now it was Pettita's turn to laugh, with that careless happy laugh which has so much of the ring of youth about it. The idea that "old Dick" should be in love with any one amused her excessively, and the supposition that the favoured individual on whom he deigned to bestow his affections should be herself, was to this very young girl too ridiculous to be entertained for a moment. Thus Pettita's thoughts were speedily withdrawn from the dreariness which had come over her when she saw her sister depart, and she was as vivacious and full of nonsense as ever, when some half-hour later Lord Avebury presented himself in the little drawing-room.

Although he was a man probably some two or three years older than Richard Griesnach, it would not have entered into Pettita's head to call him old, or to deride him in the way she did her good little self-constituted guardian, nor did she feel disposed to laugh and bandy nonsense with him, as though he were only that pleasant good-looking Sir Edward.

Pettita had, since her arrival in London, ceased to use the *sobriquet* of Prince Charming, which she had bestowed on her new acquaintance at the Squire's dance, perhaps because a good deal of the illusion had faded; and if Margaret had asked her now what she thought of Sir Edward, she would have said unhesitatingly he was a bright " chaffy " boy, who helped to make some of the hours of her life pass very pleasantly. Truly, there was no danger of Pettita falling in love with him. He was quite right when he told Mrs. Leigh she did not care a button about him, but he was piqued nevertheless.

Bertha was a little disappointed when she saw Lord Avebury enter the room unaccompanied by his nephew. "One is so seldom alone, men should always hunt in couples, like dogs; besides it is so much less compromising," was one of her aphorisms, and though of course she could not speak her thoughts, they were implied by the shrug of her shoulders. She sat back in that cosy little sofa corner of hers, and made her pretty pointed speeches in the soft purring way which fascinated every one, and which, added to the general air of comfort she knew so well how to bestow, gave her house the 'homiest' cosiest aspect to be found anywhere. In fact half an hour with Bertha Leigh so often roused a drooping courage and smoothed the rough places in a rugged career, that surely those green spots should be well watered to her advantage, whenever one feels too anxious to exhibit the prickly thorn-covered stems which were generally hidden under the rose branches she held out to most of her so-called friends.

On this occasion Lord Avebury addressed his conversation principally to Pettita. There was something about the girl's brightness and beauty which evidently pleased him, but he turned round every now and then with a sort of confidential aside to Bertha, as though to show her that she was in reality his preferred friend, and that he by no means wished her to feel jealous about any passing *petits soins* he might pay to the child who was her last toy. He need, perhaps, scarcely have troubled himself, for though Bertha hardly knew at what value to place Lord Avebury's attentions to herself, yet that he should even for a moment seriously entertain any feelings for that little chit, was an idea which would not arise without some very marked reason.

"Where's Ted?" however she asked at last, when she thought the conversation had gone on long enough without her, and she had come to a resolution to turn it into another channel, and finally to get rid of Pettita if possible.

"I have not seen him to-day," answered Lord Avebury. "He usually looks into my rooms, which are close to his own, every morning when I am in town, but there is evidently a cloud of some sort hanging over him, which I, at all events, am powerless to lift. I came back from Pau sooner than I had intended, because I was unhappy about the state in which I had left him, and affairs do not seem in the least improved."

Bertha's little shrug was slightly noticeable. She had hoped that she had something to do with Lord Avebury's speedy return.

"Young men will be young men," she said quietly. "I dare say things will shake themselves into their places with him as with others."

"A very philosophical way of viewing it, I make no doubt," he answered, laughing. "I wish I could quiet my doubts and fears as easily. If I could only get him to make a confidant of me it would be a relief, but the boy seems to avoid me at every turn. I am thinking of carrying him off down to the Abbey for a few days' hunting; we *must* get confidential when we are alone over our pipes at night."

This arrangement was in no way likely to suit Bertha, and she roused herself out of her comfortable corner.

" Two men alone at the Abbey in February ! How dull you will find it ! I should think you would end by hating each other. I cannot call that a good arrangement, Lord Avebury."

" Well, the Abbey is not a hundred miles from London. When we are tired of each other, three-quarters of an hour by train will bring us back to the haunts of beauty and pleasure ; in the meantime we can attend to a little business. I have some papers that want looking over, and Ted can help me."

" I think it very unkind of you to want to go away again so soon, but you men are so very errant in your ways there is no comprehending you. How dull we shall be! shan't we, Pettita?"

But Pettita only laughed. She had not arrived yet at considering either Lord Avebury's or his nephew's presence as essential to her life, whatever she might do later.

At this moment the door dashed open, and a new visitor broke in on the group. It was that very irrepressible Marcia Fenton, of whom Lord Avebury had almost as instinctive a horror as had Lady Bluntisfield, though this probably was the only point on which they were agreed, for Lord Avebury always stigmatised her ladyship as an inveterate old bore. He was too much of a cosmopolitan to enter *con amore* into her prejudices, as she would have had him do, because he was an aristocrat, forsooth! He liked to dawdle away some of his idle hours on the confines of Bohemia. There was a freedom about the lives of the joyous, careless band yclept Bohemians, which had for him a rare charm; but women of Marcia

Fenton's stamp were his especial aversion, they always seemed to act as an irritant, and kept him in a perpetual state of ill-temper with himself and every one else.

Impartial as by nature he was in his judgments on his fellows, he felt that he could scarcely accord her even her due, for that she was good-hearted honest and loyal her bitterest enemy must allow; but her loudness, fastness, and general vulgarity made him at times almost forget the existence of better qualities. Lord Avebury frequently thought there must be a note or two out of tune about Bertha, which he had not discovered, or she would not have encouraged this woman as an intimate friend. It never entered his unimaginative masculine brain that Marcia, notwithstanding her slang and her slap-dash, was as true as steel, while in the other's nature was mixed a very fair quantity of base alloy.

"Dear me! you look as if a thunderbolt had fallen among you. How are you, Bertha? Why, Lord Avebury, I had no idea you had come back; so this is the girl —glad to make your acquaintance dear— hope we shall be friends;" and she tapped Pettita kindly on the shoulder, and then threw herself somewhat unceremoniously into a seat.

Lord Avebury looked at Bertha and rose. He had never openly avowed his dislike to this friend of hers—perhaps he scarcely cared to assume the right,—but she knew instinctively that they were not likely to suit. It was so provoking that people always would come when they were not wanted,—when Bertha felt lonely and out of sorts, she was very glad of Marcia to cheer her, but just now she would have annihilated her on the spot if she had only dared.

"You will let me hear, then, something of your plans. You will not leave town without letting me know," she said *sotto voce* as she shook hands with her male visitor, but the words did not escape Marcia's quick ears, and she broke in with,

"Going out of town again already? Why you *are* a bird of passage. How I should like to be always on the wing!"

"I am only going to the Abbey for a few days on business," he said, more stiffly than was his usual manner with ladies.

"On business!" cried Marcia; "can't we help you? there is not much doing in London just now. Suppose we make a picnic party to the Abbey, and come and look you up some day, should you be very much surprised?"

Just a tinge of colour for a moment appeared in Bertha's usually pale face; the scheme found favour in her eyes, and she inwardly thanked Marcia for the suggestion. "These plain, outspoken people are of use sometimes in working the machinery of life," she thought.

"In the summer it would be a delightful trip for you all," said Lord Avebury, catching like a drowning man at a straw in order to put off *sine die* this threatened invasion of his house.

"In the summer, bah! we may not live till the summer."

He almost hoped she would not.

"We mean to come. Now what do you say, Bertha? Would it not be delightful?"

"Yes very, but I should be sorry to put Lord Avebury to so great an inconvenience," and she drew a pattern on the carpet with her foot, and did not look at any one.

"Pray do not think of it in that light," he answered gallantly. "I should only be too proud and happy to see you all, but I am afraid you will find the expedition a very cold and dreary one, nor is the Abbey worth seeing when you get there."

"That is modesty now," laughed Marcia, "for I always heard it was a lovely place, and had one of the finest old halls in England."

"You do the place too great honour," he said with that grand air he always assumed when not altogether pleased. "I can only repeat I shall be very happy to see you all."

"Oh! but we must make a party and you must fix the day. Invitations given in that vague general way never come to anything. What do you say, child? You have not given your opinion yet—let us have it. Would not it be jolly?"

Thus appealed to, Pettita became crimson.

"I should like it excessively," she said; "in fact, there are few things I should like better."

Lord Avebury turned and looked at her for a moment, then smiled as he said in a kind paternal way,

"So you would like to come and see my old place, Miss Pettita? Well, you shall be gratified. We will arrange this projected trip, and in the meantime let us pray for a fine day."

And for some minutes after he had left them Bertha sat silently in her old corner by the fire, and left Pettita and Marcia

to chatter away and become better acquainted without her.   She was on the
whole pleased at the idea of the expedition
to the Abbey, though scarcely gratified
that she had had so little to do in bringing
it about.

CHAPTER XV.

BREAK OF DAY.

ONCE more we take a peep at Richard Griesnach as he sits alone in that somewhat dingy room of his in the Temple. The table is littered from one end to the other with papers and pamphlets of every description, and the little man is looking very brisk and business-like, while his ready pen is moving quickly on. It is evident that the 'Educational Argus' is in full force, and a glance at Mr. Griesnach's face tells that this editorial work is, to him, no unpleasing employment. To judge from his activity as he compiles, arranges, erases, ties up, and in fact puts the first number in printing order, one would almost imagine he had been used to work all his life, and would scarcely give him credit for having been but a few weeks back a very *dilettante* scribbler indeed. Yet so it was, and such is the effect of determination of purpose, when set in motion by a vigorous mind. A weight, too, had been removed from Mr. Griesnach's thoughts,—the stage had been given up, and Pettita was safe for a while, at least, at Mrs. Leigh's; and Richard Griesnach, be it remembered, had great faith in Bertha Leigh. Altogether a light-heartedness which was very unusual to his naturally despondent nature, had come over him, so he worked away with a will, and—

"*Vogue la galère!* The 'Educational Argus' is launched at last," shouted Jenkins, as he burst into the room, and by his noisy voice almost startled Mr. Griesnach out of his chair. "Upon my word, my good fellow, I never had such hard work in my life. I thought the 'Argus' was going to be too sharp for us, indeed I did, but we have managed it,—we have managed it. A shilling a number, monthly, and all that tremendous amount of machinery required to set it in motion,—it is almost incredible! Statistical accounts of the training of street Arabs in every quarter of the civilised globe, are not easy to collect, let me tell you, and I take to myself κυδος, very great κυδος, though you are not a bad hand at knocking it into shape either."

Richard Griesnach in his present happy state of satisfaction with all the world, himself included, put out his hand, which was grasped warmly by Jenkins' huge flabby paw.

"Here are the two or three articles still remaining to be sent to the printer; had they not better be despatched at once?" said Griesnach, overjoyed at the thought that the work which for the last week had been absorbing all his time was finished *pro tem.*, and that he should now be free to go and pay the house in Belgrave Street a visit.

"Ay, ay, man! I will take them forthwith. But first of all read this glorious puff in the 'Spinning Wheel'; such an article as that ought to start us, eh?"

"The subject should of itself have sufficient weight," answered Mr. Griesnach gravely. "I hate back-door influence."

"Bah! my good fellow, we should all stand still without it. Believe me, there never yet was anything in this world accomplished without a little jobbery."

Mr. Griesnach rose and walked to the window. Jenkins, as usual, was treading on some of his corns, and he was beginning to get irritable.

"Well, it is a system I deprecate highly," he said, "and if you consider that your share in this undertaking justifies your use of any means you may have at command to push the magazine, you may, at least, accord me the privilege of being kept in ignorance of what you are doing."

"'High-flown Buckingham grows circumspect'!" shouted Mr. Jenkins, and then he burst into one of his loud, vulgar laughs.

How much there is in a laugh !—how you can tell by its very tones whether the world goes well or ill with the laugher, whether its troubles and annoyances sit carelessly or heavily on his shoulders. A man's laugh is almost the key to his inward life. Jenkins' laugh jarred unpleasantly on Richard Gries-nach, and he felt at times, when subjected to the infliction, that he could not possibly continue to coalesce with this man, but that this laugh, if nothing else, would compel him to throw up the editorship of the ' Argus '.

" Circumspect or not," he replied with a dark frown Jenkins knew how to interpret, " if we are to continue to work together, my wishes must be respected."

" All right, all right, my good fellow, don't let us quarrel whatever we do, especially, too, just when we are on the verge of success. Give me the bundle of papers. In a few days, perhaps, we may have an honester and blunter verdict on our labours than even you bargain for. Truth is not always pleasant, my good sir, not always pleasant. Ta-ta, I am off! haven't got any especial message for the printer, have you?"

Thus the edge of Richard Griesnach's seeming content was blunted, and his interview with Jenkins left him, as those interviews generally did, "riled," and out of temper with himself.

For to-day, at least, his urbanity of disposition being gone, it was useless to pay, as he had intended, a visit to that little West-end house where, just now, all his thoughts were centred. So after Jenkins' departure he put away his papers and sat down moodily. It was not that in the short conversation which had just taken place there had been anything said especially to annoy him, but it was the inward feeling that he was degrading himself by having this man for a coadjutor, which rose so forcibly before him every time they came in close contact with each other. Thus it is that irritable temperaments are easily overset. Richard Griesnach's nervous system was always highly strung; those good hours which so seldom came to him invariably raised him far above the level on which men usually find themselves when life goes brightly, while in his evil hours he sank into a perfect slough of despair, from which with difficulty, even the convictions of his wiser and more trained self could scarcely raise him.

Jarred, then, and set out of tune by his recent interview with the man with whom fate had elected he should be brought so closely in contact, he felt inclined to give way to dark thoughts and despairing fancies, instead of rousing himself to action, and smiling at his partner's shortcomings as he would have done had his tone of mind been a healthier one. He reached a favourite book from a shelf close by, and having wheeled his chair near the fire, seemed as though he were going to give himself up to that hour of dreamland which none but an overworked mind, as his had been of late, knows how to appreciate. Let the drones fancy they have the best of life, it is only the workers who can truly value the sweets of repose.

Richard Griesnach's hour of rest, however, belonged to that list of " unaccomplished desires " which usually forms so long a one in most human histories,—and well, perhaps, it is for us that such is the case.

He had scarcely lain back, dreaming over, not reading his book for five minutes, when his eye casually fell on Captain St. Orme's unopened desk. He had been too busy ever since his return from Woodlands to do more than cast an occasional glance at it as it stood on a side-table. This afternoon then, the 'Argus' being despatched and his own thoughts being ready to take a morbid turn, was the very time to unlock that relic of the past, and to penetrate into some of the secrets which, for all he knew, would perhaps have been better buried with those who had passed away.

It is a strange medley, that collection of papers and scraps which we most of us gather so eagerly together in life, and hide so carefully from other eyes but our own, forgetting that the day must come sooner or later when they will either bring sorrow to a loving heart, or derision to cold scornful eyes. There are few dead men's treasures which fall into the reverential hands that Captain St. Orme's did. Poor proud Margaret! it was well too that the opening of that desk had passed away from her, for there lay revealed the history of her mother's early career, the knowledge of which would have bowed her down with grief, and she had quite sorrows and troubles enough of her own just now to keep the balance of her life even, she scarcely wanted this new one to add to their weight.

Richard Griesnach sat and mused long with the record of how Mrs. St. Orme's

early days had been passed lying open
before him on the table. He remembered
how angrily annoyed he had been with his
friend when he first became aware of the
marriage he had contracted,—then his
thoughts passed on to that one only time
when he had seen the wife, and how in his
heart he had freely forgiven St. Orme for
his folly. For the image of the Lima
beauty had dwelt on through years in
Richard Griesnach's mind, even till he saw
it reproduced in her child, and the cry for
love which he had hoped was silenced for
ever in his breast had made itself heard
again more loudly than ever when he
beheld Pettita.

"If she could only bear with me and be
happy with me," was his wail, as he sat
there with the history of her father and
mother's early loves in his hand; and
when he turned over the pages and read
the whole account as Captain St. Orme had
written it down day by day, as it all
happened, he wondered how it was that

he could have passed the severe verdict he
had once done on his friend's "foolhardy
rashness."

How strange are the issues of events!

Years had swept on their course, the
child of that foolish union had grown to
woman's estate, and he, the grizzly man
who for some years now had had no thought
of a home life beyond those Temple chambers, was roused from his selfish cares, and
his whole nature was aglow as he hoped
that the twin-born happiness for which all
mortals long, was not to be for him altogether a blank and a desert.

> "Shine! shine! shine!
>   Pour down your warmth, great sun!
>   While we bask, we two together,
>   Two together!
>   Winds blow south, or winds blow north,
>   Day come white, or night keep black,
>   Home, or rivers and mountains from home,
>   Singing all time, minding no time,
>   If we two but keep together."

Were it not for dreams, what would some

of our lives be ? The active mind works off its annoyances and its vexations in action, the contemplative nature dreams and makes a bright future for itself, in a world peopled by its own imaginings. Dreamy then was Richard Griesnach's mood as he sat alone in that solitary room, with the cold spring winds soughing in the narrow courts, and making but a dreary accompaniment to the bright picture he was painting for himself on the worn canvas of that old bygone love story.

Those who had noted him as a shrewd, keen-sighted man, who could hit hard at both public and private grievances with a vigorous and unyielding pen, might not have understood this reversed side which his nature now presented ; yet so it is, every highly developed point of character has its strong opposite.

At last he shook himself back from that happy land of romance, and went on with his investigation of the contents of the desk. There seemed to be little of particular interest, though many old letters brought vividly back to Richard Griesnach's mind the recollection of days now long gone by, which the two friends, who had been as brothers, had passed happily together.

The search was well-nigh over, and save for the finding of that one particular document, which he wished to keep from the girls' knowledge, it had yielded no especial information, till on a sudden by an accident his hand touched a spring of the existence of which he was unaware, and a secret drawer flew open. It contained two or three old papers tied together with a string.

At almost the first glance, Richard Griesnach saw that they must have been there for years,—long before the desk came into the possession of Captain St. Orme. They referred to people of whom he had never heard, and had not the instincts which had been awakened in him when he had been studying for the Bar caused him to read them steadily to the end, he would probably at once have thrown them in the fire as worthless and irrelevant. Something, however, on a sudden seemed to rouse him. He no longer perused the old papers as a mere matter of duty. All his acuteness was brought into service; the man of dreams gave place to the lawyer, and as he at last put them all down before him on the table, there was a feverish look on his pale intelligent face, a fire burning in his keen eyes, which showed without words how thoroughly he had been aroused, how that in the short half-hour that he had been reading there, a new epoch had arisen which must inevitably change the current of several lives. But Richard Griesnach's thoughts had evidently been carried far back into past years, for—·

"St. Orme, my poor old friend!" were the words he almost inaudibly spoke as his long thin fingers nervously wandered over the papers.

Then the recollection of the younger

generation seemed to spring up before him, and as his lips framed Pettita's name he started hastily to his feet, as though he would seek her immediately. Poor Margaret with her patient anxious watchings—was she always to be quite forgotten?

But Mr. Griesnach did not immediately follow his first impulse. He took the papers up once more, and reperused them. He could scarcely trust to his own judgment in his present excited state,—he must have an opinion.

To whom should he turn? To Jenkins? He was practical, business-like, and less likely to be imposed upon than he was himself, notwithstanding his greater learning and more refined perceptions.

A few minutes more and the little man with his precious bundle of papers in his hand, might be seen hobbling through the courts in search of Jenkins,—for the first time, perhaps, in his' life, impatiently desiring to find him, and feeling as it were that in his hands lay a great issue, **for** according to the verdict Jenkins **should** pass, **Mr.** Griesnach felt much in the future might shape itself.

END OF VOL. I.

PRINTED BY TAYLOR AND CO.,
LITTLE QUEEN STREET, LINCOLN'S INN FIELDS.